FADE

Into You,
Into Me,
Into Always

KATE DAWES

Cover Image File licensed by www.depositphotos.com/Zoooom

Paperback edition: October 2012
Also available as an e-book

ISBN-13: 978-1480008908

ISBN-10: 1480008907

For SJ,
the inspiration for this novel,
and for the readers,
who made all of this possible.

FADE INTO YOU

ONE

I had been living and working in Los Angeles for only three weeks when I met the man who would change everything for me. I'd heard his name before, but only during the last few weeks of working in and around Hollywood.

As a regular girl, fresh out of Ohio State University, a Midwestern transplant to Tinsel Town, I'd never heard of Max Dalton before. Maybe I would have, if I'd paid attention to movie credits and caught his name on the screen. He was a writer and producer. I plead guilty—actually ignorant—to not knowing who he was before I began seeing his name on documents and hearing his name around the office.

Before walking into his office, I'd never seen him, though. I accompanied my boss, Kevin Anderson, to the meeting. Kevin was trying to get one of our agency's clients cast in a new movie, and Max Dalton was the producer.

Max Dalton's appearance wouldn't have been such a surprise if I'd bothered to Google him and do a little research before the meeting. But I hadn't. Chalk it up to my being new, but it was something that just hadn't occurred to me. My focus was the presentation of our client.

Most of the hour we were in Max Dalton's office, I sat there staring at him, unable to focus on the matter at hand. Max Dalton stood about six feet tall, with broad shoulders and a trim waist. It wasn't a bodybuilder's physique, much to my delight, but he did have that V-shape thing going on. I suppose the clothing he wore didn't hurt, either. Dark gray slacks, and a white button-down shirt with the first two or three buttons open, revealing smooth and evenly tanned skin.

His hair was just long enough to get messed up if a certain girl had the chance to run her fingers through it. At the beginning of the meeting it appeared to be slicked back and I wondered if he was one of those guys who overdo it with the gel. But as the hour progressed, it started to dry, and I figured maybe he'd just gotten out of the shower in the private bathroom in his office. Maybe he'd been working out before the meeting, and in the thirty minutes I'd spent in the waiting room, he was in that bathroom, in the shower, soaping up....

See? That's why I was so distracted. And, honestly, it kind of pissed me off. I had come to this town to work, establish myself, start my life. I couldn't afford to be so lacking in self-control in any area of life, let alone with men. I'd had my share of man troubles, and when I arrived in LA, I'd promised myself that I'd say goodbye to all that for a long, long time.

Work. I was here to work. I kept trying to tell myself that, repeating it like some mantra over and over and over...

"What do you think, Ms. Rowland?"

It would have been bad enough if those words had come out of Kevin's mouth. But they came out of Max's. Either way, though, there I was sitting next to my boss and across from a Hollywood mogul, caught totally off guard because I hadn't been paying attention.

I was already looking at Max, so refocusing was just a matter of moving my gaze from his lips to his eyes. I'd already noticed that they appeared to be a mixture of gray and light blue, but this time I saw that one eyebrow was raised to punctuate the question he had directed at me.

I didn't have the first clue about the context of the question. It was a prime opportunity for me to appear completely idiotic and useless. But there was no way I was going to let that happen.

Without missing a beat I said, "With all due respect, Mr. Dalton, I appreciate being asked for my input, but Mr.

Anderson is the pro here." I said it with a smile and a glance toward Kevin Anderson.

Luckily, Kevin picked up where I left off and launched into his closing argument in favor of our client.

Saved by a little wit. It doesn't happen often for me, but when it does, it always seems to happen when it really counts.

This is the part where you'd think I would have gotten control of myself and paid attention to what was being said. But as Kevin spoke, I stared at Max. Staring was okay; after all, he could have thought I was simply watching his reaction to Kevin's spiel. But that wasn't at all what I was doing.

I'm a Midwestern girl. Fairly normal. Pretty tame, actually. I'm not a virgin, and I've had my share of sex. I've never watched pornography, though, which made it even more strange that such images were in my head. They were like the flash scenes in a movie, the kind where the light flickers and increases and you catch a couple of seconds of the action. In this case, the action was me, facedown, with Max behind me…the kind of fucking that rips the sheets right off the bed.

The few times he glanced at me, my paranoia worried that he could see what I was thinking. Crazy, I know.

When the meeting was over, Max rose and came around the desk. He shook Kevin's hand, placing his other hand on the back of Kevin's arm. I'd learned in a Psych class that it was a show of power and dominance. I wasn't surprised to see it in a Hollywood meeting.

Max looked at me. "Ms. Rowland, it was a pleasure meeting you."

"Thank you, Mr. Dalton."

I reached to offer and handshake as he was saying, "Please call me Max."

His hand was large and strong, and he gave a firm yet warm handshake. If I wanted to be melodramatic about it, I would say a tiny bolt of electricity jumped between our hands. But nothing like that happened. The smooth firmness and inviting warmth of his hand was thrilling enough.

"Okay, Max. Please call me Olivia."

He smiled, said, "Olivia it is," and we all turned toward the doors.

Kevin went through first, stepping out into the reception area, where he quickly struck up a conversation with Max's secretary. "It seems like we talk on the phone almost every day…"

Their conversation faded out as I felt Max's hand at the small of my back. He leaned over my shoulder, his mouth close to my ear. "Nice dodge in there."

I turned my head. "What do you mean?"

"When I asked what you thought. Very nicely handled, Olivia."

"I don't—" I started to lie but he interrupted me.

"It's okay." He laughed. "Really. I'm just giving you a hard time. We'll talk soon, I'm sure."

I felt the blood rush to my face. Great. Blushing in a professional setting.

Kevin faced us again and thanked Max once more for the meeting and I couldn't have been happier that we were on our way out of there.

The ride back to the office from the studio was a short one. As Kevin drove he kept saying he thought the meeting went well and that Jacqueline Mathers, our actress client, was almost sure to get the part and that meant a big deal to the agency.

At a stop light he looked over at me. "By the way, that was great what you did in there. I appreciate it."

"What's that?"

“The way you deferred to me. I mean, you’re familiar enough with the issue to comment, otherwise I wouldn’t have brought you along at all, but…well, thanks.”

“You’re welcome.”

I’d been a little worried that he knew the real reason I had deferred to him. Max had sure picked up on it. But Kevin thought I was just being a good assistant and letting the boss handle the matter. Good enough.

The rest of the day went well, though much of it was consumed with thoughts about Max Dalton. I was sure I’d never before seen such a perfect example of what people mean when they say a man can be beautiful.

I’d always thought it a feminine adjective, and I suppose there were famous men I’d seen who would have been worthy of it, but it had never occurred to me before I saw Max. I couldn’t help but think he should have been in the movies rather than the behind-the-scenes guy. Why was that? Had he pursued acting and not liked it? Failed?

Toward the end of the day I used my phone to Google his name. I felt a little paranoid about getting caught doing some research on him after the meeting—something I should have done well before.

The first result that came up was his IMDb listing. There was one picture of him, taken at a red carpet event. It wasn't a close-up and didn't do him justice at all. I scrolled down to the section that listed his credits: three as a writer, nine as producer. No acting or directing credits.

I would have been in even greater awe of him during the meeting had I known then that he had written one of my favorite movies. He'd even been nominated for an Oscar.

Whoa. This guy was a bigger deal than I realized, and I suddenly felt like a fool for not knowing. Although, Kevin hadn't made a point of it. All he had told me was that this was one of the most important meetings he'd probably have all year. I figured it was just because we were pitching Jaqueline Mathers. Now I knew it was also because we were meeting with a true Hollywood big shot.

I scrolled back up to the top of the page and saw his birth date. He was only twenty-nine. It had to be unusual to reach his level of success at such a young age. He had seemed easy-going, friendly, and not snobbish or hung up on himself. Especially with the light-hearted comment he made to me as I was leaving his office.

By the end of the day I was completely enthralled with Max Dalton, and I had no idea how much pleasure and pain it would bring me in the coming months.

As I left the office my nerves were on edge. Not only because of Max, but because I was so new to my job, new to the entire business of Hollywood, and already I was a major part of what could be a major deal with an up and coming star and a blockbuster movie. The waiting game was on—Kevin had told me we'd probably know something next week.

To ease my anxiety, I put the top down on my new Volkswagen Beetle and let the California air blow through my hair as I drove home. The car was my first big purchase in life. I had pooled all my college graduation money for the down payment. It was a great ride all the way from Ohio to California.

When I got home I opened the door to find Krystal straddling a guy on our couch.

Krystal Sherman was two years older than me, and had been in California for three years now. She was really more my sister Grace's friend, but when she found out I was headed to southern California she offered to let me stay there as long as I needed.

She was one of the few people who knew the whole truth about why I wanted to get the hell out of Ohio. Most people thought it was just about wanting a fresh start after college. That's also what most people thought about my breaking up with Chris Cooper after three years of serious dating.

What most people didn't know was that during our senior year at Ohio State, Chris cheated on me with no less than three girls. That alone was grounds for dumping him, but there was more—things I didn't even tell my parents. The only people who knew the whole story were my sister Grace, and Krystal.

Krystal had come to Hollywood to pursue an acting career, but like so many others, she was a full-time waitress while she waited to be discovered. To her credit, she hadn't asked me to do her any favors and try to get Kevin's agency to rep her. She seemed determined to do it on her own merit.

When she heard the door open, she turned around. "Oh, hey."

She didn't move off the guy. They were both clothed, and I felt bad that I had walked in while something was just getting started. Sure, she could have been doing this in her room, but it was her condo, so I couldn't complain.

"Hey, sorry." I turned my back to them as I closed the door.

"No worries."

I turned and started to walk through the den and to my bedroom, but Krystal stopped me.

"This is Marco," she said, looking from me to him.

I smiled. "Hi."

He looked back at me through heavily-lidded eyes. "What's up?"

I looked back at Krystal, who had rested her head on his shoulder, still straddling him. "I'll just be in my room."

She slid off him. "No, no, it's okay. We were just figuring out what to do for dinner."

I'd had moments of indecision before about where to eat, but had never thought of trying to answer the question by straddling a cute guy. Maybe I was missing out.

"Any ideas?" she said.

"You're off tonight?"

"Oh, yeah. They had too many servers scheduled and called and asked me if I wanted off."

That had happened at least five times in the three weeks since I'd arrived in LA. I wondered how Krystal afforded to take so much time off, but it was none of my business.

Marco wasn't paying any attention to the conversation. His eyes were on Krystal. More specifically, on her boobs, which were straining against the tight t-shirt she was wearing. I got the feeling he didn't really care about dinner at the moment.

We finally decided to go to a little sushi place. Unfortunately, Marco joined us. I wanted to tell Krystal all about Max. But I didn't want to bring it up with Marco there. I didn't know him. In fact, I'd never heard Krystal talk about him, either.

After dinner, she said she was going back to his place and would probably be home late.

On the way home, I wondered what I'd do with the rest of my night. I could call Grace, but it was too soon to tell my sister about Max. She would only have been negative about it, telling me to be careful around "those Hollywood types," as she and my parents like to say.

I spent the rest of the evening watching a few of Max's movies on Netflix and wondering when, or even *if*, I'd see him again.

TWO

I didn't see Max the next week. I did talk to him once when Kevin asked me to get him on the line.

Jacqueline called every day to ask if we'd heard anything about her getting the part in the movie. Kevin assured her that the wait time was normal and by Thursday he had instructed me to tell her he was in a meeting, which meant I had to take over the comforting and reassuring.

One night, after dinner and over a glass of wine, I told Krystal about having met Max.

"Max Dalton?"

"Yeah."

"Who's that?"

I laughed. "I didn't know who he was, either, until I looked it up. And this was after I met him." I told her the whole story about the meeting.

"Oh, yeah. I know his movies. Hell yeah. I just didn't know the name."

We were in the majority. According to Kevin, and confirmed by my own experience, people rarely know the writers and producers, save for a few big names.

"And," I said, "the worst part is, he's hot as hell."

"Why is that the worst part?"

"Because I have to work with him and I can't focus when I'm around him or when he's on the phone."

Krystal swallowed the last of her drink, and shook her head. "You're in Hollywood, honey. Get ready to be smitten with a lot of people."

Krystal called the office on Friday afternoon and said, "Let's go to Vegas!"

"What? When?"

"This weekend."

I wasn't up for a trip anywhere, let alone to Vegas. "For what?"

"For *what*? It's Vegas, baby! We don't need a reason beyond that. But if you really do need a reason, I think it would be a great way to celebrate your first month out here working in the biz."

Krystal was the only person I knew who called it "the biz." It made me wonder if she was trying too hard. Maybe that's why she hadn't been able to get representation.

I looked at the clock on my computer—4:16. "That sounds like fun, but I don't think I have any Vegas attire, first of all, and—"

"Okay, you're looking for excuses not to go, but you're going."

"Says who?"

Her voice echoed, like she'd walked into the bathroom. "Says me. It's part of initiation. Come on. It's just two days. Trust me, you won't regret it."

A few seconds of silence passed, then I thought of something. "Who's going?"

"Just me and you."

I was glad to hear that her new friend Marco wasn't going. There was something about that guy I didn't like, something about the way he looked at Krystal, and the way he looked at me when Krystal left the room. He didn't talk much, but he sure liked to stare a lot. He was unsettling, to say the least. I couldn't figure out what she saw in him, and I hadn't asked. It was none of my business.

She pressed on making her case. "I'll pay for the gas and all the other stuff. It's all on me."

"You don't have to do that."

"I know I don't *have* to. I want to."

"All right," I said. "When do you want to leave?"

By nine o'clock that night, we were two hours into the roughly four-hour drive to Vegas. We had great travel weather, and little traffic, although we did get stuck behind an RV for a while somewhere in Nevada that slowed us down.

"So how's Grace?" Krystal asked at one point during the drive.

It made me realize I hadn't talked to my sister in over a week, a record for us. I was just so busy and so preoccupied I hadn't gotten around to calling her. Of course, she hadn't called me, either, so I didn't feel guilty. Two-way streets, and all that.

"I guess she's okay," I said.

"You guess?"

I explained how I hadn't talked to Grace lately.

Krystal reached to turn the stereo down. "I think she'd like it here."

"Ha. I doubt it."

"I know. I just mean, if she gave it a chance. If she gave *anything* a chance."

This was my sister we were talking about, and Krystal's tone had a little too much sarcastic negativity to it, so I just shrugged and said, "Yeah."

What she was referring to was my sister having taken the same route as my mother. Married young, two kids, stay-at-home mom, no apparent ambition outside of those things. Honestly, I can respect that. I just wish Grace had given the world a look before she settled down. She was only two years older than me, but she acted like she was thirty years older. She acted like my mom. And seeing as how I already had two parents who'd like to make every life decision for me, the last thing I needed was a third one.

And, really, she should have known that. The pressure I'd felt to become Mrs. Chris Cooper was like a slow, constant suffocation. Several times after I broke up with him, my mom had pushed me so close to spilling the whole truth about what Chris had done. What stopped me from doing it was the sense that it would have only made them even more protective of me. And with the town being as small as it was, there was every chance in the world that my story would get around, and people wouldn't believe me. Instead, they'd rally behind Chris Cooper, all –American church-going guy and former quarterback of the two-time champion football team at our high school. My only choice was to keep my head down and just leave.

"Oh, well," Krystal was saying. "Her loss."

"Yeah."

That conversation wouldn't have gotten far even if I hadn't stopped it, because it wasn't long before we saw the lights of Vegas twinkling in the distance—almost beckoning people to come there. I felt the pull of excitement.

We got to our hotel, handed the keys to the valet, and walked into what I can only describe as sensory overload.

Lights. Music. Gaming machines clinking and humming and buzzing and ringing. People everywhere. People looking sad. People looking elated. People looking like they were in a trance. I was definitely part of the latter group.

We went straight up to our room, freshened up, and got dressed for our first night in Vegas. I had on my favorite little black dress, black heels, silver hoop earrings, and a silver necklace with a Gehry orchid pendant—a gift from my mother.

"I don't look like a hooker, do I?" Krystal said.

I poked my head out of the bathroom, putting on my earrings. "Hell, no, girl. You look sexy."

I looked at myself again in the mirror. I actually felt kind of sexy, myself.

We were downstairs and in the casino by midnight. It had gotten busier in the relatively short time we were upstairs.

"This is when Vegas really gets started," Krystal told me as we exited the elevator.

While she had insisted on paying for everything, I wouldn't let her give me any gambling money. I appreciated her footing the bill for our stay but there was no way I was going to lose her money. I felt more comfortable losing my own.

Which is exactly what happened, and in short order. The roulette wheel had sucked me in and taken my conservative gambling budget for the night. After that, it was just drinks—three glasses of wine—and people watching, an endlessly fascinating form of entertainment in a place like Las Vegas.

The last person I expected to be watching was Max, but there he was, standing at the craps table. Looking stunning, of course. He had two-day stubble on his otherwise smooth face, and he wore black slacks, black blazer, and a blue shirt, no tie. He looked taller than I thought this time. Maybe it was just the contrast of his powerful frame next to a half dozen or so other men. And women. Who could miss those women? They were all blondes, and they were all hanging on him between rolls of the dice.

I thought back to Krystal's earlier question about looking like a hooker and realized I had nothing to worry about. These women looked more the part. Maybe that's what they were. My estimation of Max suddenly dropped a little.

I stood there for maybe five minutes, watching the spectacle, and then Krystal appeared beside me.

"Fucking blackjack. It's rigged!"

Without taking my eyes off of Max, I said, "Lost big, huh?"

"Yup. I'm usually better at… what are you staring at?"

"Not *what*," I said. "Who."

"Okay. Who?" She turned to stand beside me and look where I was looking. "He's hot."

"Told you so. That's Max Dalton."

Krystal held the wineglass tipped at her mouth. "Oh, wow."

"Yeah. Wow doesn't quite cover it."

"Look at those shameless bitches around him."

By now, that's pretty much all I was looking at. Some of them appeared to be one step away from dropping their dresses right there in the open casino and letting him have his way with them.

"Let's go somewhere else," I said.

Krystal started to say something about a game called Keno when I looked at Max one more time. I shouldn't have. Then I wouldn't have locked eyes with him, and he wouldn't have been waving me over to where he was.

"Oh, no," I said under my breath.

"It doesn't have to be Keno. We could find a—"

"No," I said. "He saw me."

Krystal looked across the way to Max. "He's calling you over there."

I knew I should go. We had business to do with him and ignoring him wouldn't exactly be a smart business decision. A lot was riding on his decision about whether to cast Jacqueline or not.

"Go!" Krystal gave me a nudge. "I want to see the looks on those chicks' faces when you get there."

I looked at her. "Thanks a lot."

She smiled and said, "You can always count on me for support."

As I started walking toward Max, it was like someone had turned down the volume on the entire casino. My eyes were fixed on him. It was my first experience with tunnel vision. I shouldered my way through the throng of women around him. They were reluctant to give me room until Max extended his hand and I reached up to take it.

"Hello, Olivia."

"Mr. Max. I mean, hi, Max. Sorry. You told me not to call you Mr. Dalton, and I..." Jesus, how embarrassing. I was sounding so dumb, I didn't even finish the sentence. I decided to just shut up.

"Actually, I kind of like Mr. Max."

I appreciated his sense of humor. It put me at ease a little.

"What are you drinking?"

"Wine. Chardonnay."

He flagged down a waitress and told her to bring another Chardonnay. "And another White Russian for me."

The waitress said, "Yes, sir," and when she walked away Max turned back to me.

"Thanks," I said.

"Olivia, do you know anything about craps?"

I looked at the confusing table, then up at the dealer. I'd never played it and figured there was no way I would figure it out in the next two seconds, especially with the wine cruising through my bloodstream and the temperature rising from being in this situation.

"I'll take that as a no," Max said.

"You would be correct."

"No problem." He reached down to the table and picked up the dice. "You're just here for luck, anyway."

"I'm not sure I'm the type of luck you want." I stopped just short of telling him I had blown my nightly gambling budget in under thirty minutes.

Max eyed me up and down, then up again. "I think you're exactly what I want."

My face flushed. I felt the heat start in my chest and rise up my neck. What I needed after hearing that was a cold glass of water. Not to drink; to throw in my face and wake me from this bizarre experience.

The waitress returned with our drinks. Max put a hundred dollar bill on her tray and thanked her. He handed me the glass of wine, raised his tumbler of White Russian and said, "To Vegas." We clinked our glasses together, and as I sipped my wine I let my eyes roam the crowd around us. The women definitely were not liking what they were seeing. I imagined some of them had spent hours clinging to him like lint, and here I was, a girl who to them appeared to come out of nowhere, and now was the object of Max's flirting. Intense flirting. Maybe more than that....

He brought his fist up between our faces and opened his fingers, revealing the dice. "Blow on these."

My eyebrows shot up my forehead. It didn't take a dirty mind to come up with all kinds of wicked interpretations of his words, but it wasn't even so much what he said. It was how he said it. There was a commanding tone to the words, carried on the deep resonance of his intensely male voice.

"Go ahead," he urged as I hesitated.

He held his hand up close to my face. I took in a sharp breath, then blew on the dice, and a split second later he launched them down the table. When they finally stopped, I saw that each had landed on two.

“Hard way four,” the dealer called out, and scooped up the dice.

People around us cheered.

Max looked at me. “Nice work.”

“That’s good, I guess?”

Over the next fifteen minutes, he tried to explain the game to me. I understood very little of it. But Max was very good. In the time I stood next to him, he must have won fifty thousand dollars. It was just one more aspect of the night that had my head spinning.

Krystal had been hanging around in the crowd, and when we stopped playing I introduced her to Max.

“Krystal, very nice to meet you. Max Dalton.”

She smiled as they shook hands. “I’m a huge fan of your work.”

“Thank you.”

This is the part where I thought Krystal would drop a subtle—or maybe not so subtle—hint that she was an aspiring actress, but she didn’t.

So I did. But she stopped me before I got too far into it.

"I'm going to leave you two alone," she said suddenly. "Mr. Dalton, it was really nice meeting you." When she looked at me I saw that she was really uncomfortable. "I'll see you later in the room. Or...whenever. Have fun!"

And with that, she was off to somewhere else in the casino, leaving me standing there with Max, wondering just what the hell I was supposed to do now.

THREE

Max and I ended up in a little bar area that was enclosed by glass. The room was filled with live piano music. The quiet was a nice respite from the incessant energy of the casino floor.

I had my fifth glass of wine. Not being a big drinker, I probably should have stopped at four. Maybe three. But there I was, sipping the fifth one in a matter of just two hours, while Max enjoyed another White Russian.

Just what the hell I thought I was doing, I have no idea. I was in over my head spending time alone with a guy like this. I thought there would be a lot of business talk, but in less than ten minutes he was asking me questions I wouldn't have predicted in a million years.

"Why are you single, Olivia?"

"Maybe I'm not." I decided to go the playful route, rather than tell him the truth: *Oh, my only long-term boyfriend cheated on me three times and then freaked out one night, basically scaring me out of town, and I haven't dated since, and by the way I've had many sleepless nights wondering if I'll ever really trust a man again because Chris had hidden his true dark self so well, even though I thought I knew his soul. Still interested?*

A smile curled the edges of his mouth. "You don't have a ring on your finger." He took my hand and his thumb caressed the bare place where a ring would have been. "And you didn't come here with a guy."

I looked up from my hand and met his gaze. "This could be a girls' only weekend. Get away from the boyfriends for a few days."

"Right." His eyes expressed his amusement. He could see right through me.

"And who are you with?"

He looked around the bar, then back at me. "You."

With Max touching me, and with the way he said "you," my nerves were tingling. I crossed one leg over the other, and the pressure between my legs sparked a ripple of excitement. I'd never been this turned on just sitting with a guy before.

Then again, I'd never been just sitting around with anyone who came anywhere close to rivaling Max Dalton's sex appeal.

This was a bad idea. I needed to change the subject or get the hell out of there. Getting involved with Max was something that could be bad business. And it might even be worse to let him continue hitting on me and then turn him down. I didn't just have to protect myself; I had to protect my job.

I politely thanked him for the glass of wine and stood.

"Got another hot date?" he asked.

"Is that what this was?"

"It could have been."

"It was good to see you, Max. But I really need to get going. I'm exhausted from the trip and…from the last couple of hours of this." I motioned to the casino floor.

"At least let me take you back to your room."

"All right," I said.

We made our way to the elevator and I couldn't help but think he might try something on the ride up. Luckily, the elevator was crowded. Unluckily, we were squished together, with Max right behind me. I could feel his hard cock against my ass.

Opening the door to our hotel room, I said, "Krystal might be here. So, thanks again."

He held the door open and looked over my head into the room. "She's not here. How about a goodnight kiss?"

I shook my head. "I'm sorry—"

Before I could finish the sentence, he leaned toward me, swiftly, pressing his mouth to mine. His tongue parted my lips and slid into my mouth. He tasted faintly of Kahlua. The two-day stubble was rough and masculine, a feeling I hadn't had against my face in a too long. Max smelled of expensive cologne and it made me want to bury my face in his neck and inhale him.

I knew I shouldn't have, but I let him keep kissing me. And I let him step into the room, over the threshold of the doorway, and all bets were off by then. The door closed behind him with a snap, and he was walking me backward as his tongue explored my mouth.

The backs of my legs touched the bed and I started to fall to my back. He swiftly moved one arm around me, caught me, and lowered me gently onto the bed.

My legs parted and the little black dress rode up, exposing more of my thighs than I'd planned on showing anyone tonight. Max's hand wrapped around the back of one of my thighs and he settled in between my legs. Through my panties, and through the fabric of his slacks, I felt his erection press against me.

"Wait," I said, pulling my mouth away from his. "We can't do this."

"Can't make out on your bed?" He kissed me deeply again.

I put my hands on his arms to push him away. But once I felt the firm biceps, I just squeezed them. He groaned. "You like them?"

I did, but I wasn't going to say it out loud.

"Max, I'm serious."

He stopped kissing me, stopped rubbing himself against me, but stayed where he was. "Me, too. I want you, Olivia. Right here. Now."

He lowered his head and his tongue was in my mouth, licking my tongue.

I closed my eyes and then my fingers were running through his hair. I could hear my heart beating in my ears as the hot air from Max's heavy breathing heated our kiss even more.

His hand stroked my thigh possessively, his fingers brushing the edge of my panties. He pulled away from the kiss and looked down as he raised the hem of my dress higher, exposing my bare legs and silk panties, which by now had started to become wet.

"God, Olivia. You're so sexy." His voice was so low it was almost just vibration at that point, our bodies so close it was as though I was absorbing the sounds he was making.

The situation was dizzyingly hot.

He pushed against me, letting me feel how hard his cock was. I raised my hips to meet him. I looked into his eyes and saw a primal craving. My mind swam in the fantasy of being the object of his desire.

Max brought his hand up to my shoulder. One finger slipped under the strap of my dress.

This was it. He was about to get me naked. There'd be no going back after that. Not just because he wouldn't want to stop, but because I wouldn't want to either.

This was bad, bad news. It was rife with potential to ruin our business relationship. It could ruin everything. It could ruin *me*, professionally and emotionally.

On top of that, there was a huge risk that his Hollywood lifestyle found him in situations like this all the time. Once that unfortunate nugget of doubt and fear entered my mind, I couldn't get rid of it. I didn't want to be another mark on his scorecard.

I needed to stop him before this went further.

When I heard the door opening, I looked up and my eyes met Max's. He said, "Fuck," and was off me, moving to a sitting position on the bed.

Krystal popped into the room before I could rearrange myself. I was just rising up from lying down, my dress was still hiked up to my hips. Embarrassing, yes, but a small price to pay for her providing me an easier way out of this situation.

Krystal stopped in her tracks. "Oops. Sorry. I'll leave."

Max didn't say anything.

"No, no, it's okay," I said, pulling my dress back down my legs to a more respectable length.

Max looked at me. "It is?"

I nodded my head and looked at Krystal. "Max was just leaving."

Max stood.

I said, "I'll walk you out."

Krystal stepped into the bathroom. "Guys, seriously, if you want me to leave…"

"You're fine," I said.

When we got out into the hallway, Max backed me up against the wall and kissed me, his tongue licking lusciously through my mouth.

"That was a close call," he said.

"Yeah. Good thing she came in."

"No, not good at all. I'm not giving up on this. I'm not giving up on *you*, Olivia."

I crossed my arms over my chest. Probably more defensive than I needed to be. "It would probably be a good idea if you did."

Max leaned in, his face barely two inches from mine. "Do I seem like the kind of guy who doesn't go after exactly what he wants?" He kissed me again for a solid minute, then took a step back, eyed me up and down, and said, "You're perfect."

Then he just started walking down the hall, not looking back. I stood there silently, stunned by what had just happened to me over the last couple of hours.

When Max turned the corner down the hallway I fell back against the wall and said under my breath: "So. Are. You."

FOUR

Krystal gave me shit about the whole thing the rest of the weekend. We spent Saturday walking around Las Vegas, eating a killer lunch at a cheap buffet. Indulgent, not very healthy, and just what I wanted after the crazy night I'd just had.

I didn't see Max again until Sunday morning. Krystal and I were checking out of the hotel, standing at the reception desk. Since the weekend was her treat, she was handling the bill and I was free to look around.

Max was standing at the entrance to the hotel restaurant, dressed in casual clothing. He had his Ray Bans on, so I couldn't see his eyes. I figured he might have a hangover and he was shielding them from the light.

Next to him stood a statuesque blonde in a red dress. She had her back to me so I couldn't make out her face. She stood with one foot crossed over the other, her ankles locked. She wore five-inch heels that showed off her calf muscle definition. She seemed to be doing most of the talking.

At one point she put her hand on Max's shoulder.

I hated the fact that seeing that gesture made my stomach turn. It seemed like I didn't have grounds to be jealous. After all, I was the one who rejected him and ended our night. But I resented the fact that I *had* to end it. I knew I'd done the right thing, but still I hated it.

Max had told me he wasn't giving up, that he wasn't the type of guy who didn't pursue what he wanted. I had no reason to think that wasn't true, but seeing him with that woman was like a slap in the face. Of course he went after what he pursued. Of course he got what he wanted. And he probably did want me. It's just that I wasn't the only one. Exactly as I had predicted to myself when he was on top of me in the hotel room the other night.

I really needed to let this go....

Sunday was my usual check-in day with my parents, so I called them when we got back to LA.

They were on separate phones at their house and when I told them what I'd done that weekend, there was a short span of silence before my mom said, "Harold, did you hear what she said?"

"Yeah."

"Well, aren't you going to say anything?"

"I thought you were."

This was usual for my parents. They were both very conservative and demanding of Grace and me, but the lectures usually fell to my mom.

She said, "They call it 'Sin City.' Did you know that, Olivia?"

"Yes, Mom, I've heard that before."

Oh, if only she knew how close I came to sinning with Max.

"You know that, Harold, right?" It was like my mom was scolding him, too.

I shut down that part of the conversation by asking about their favorite topic of discussion, Claire, my niece. They recounted each and every little thing Claire was doing as she approached her first birthday, and my mom said, "You'll see her soon. Thanksgiving, right?"

I told her that I was definitely coming home for Christmas, but wasn't sure about Thanksgiving yet. This touched off a ten minute debate, and by the end of it I couldn't have been more ready to end that exhausting call.

I went out into the den and found Krystal lying on the couch watching TV. She was riveted to an argument between two of the Kardashian sisters. I sat down in one of the chairs and watched for a few minutes, but it was annoying and I was able to block it out with thoughts of Max.

When the show went to commercial, Krystal muted the television. "What's wrong?"

I snapped out of my daydream. "Nothing."

"Lie."

"It's just…I don't know."

She sat up and faced me. "It's Mr. Hollywood, isn't it?"

I pulled my feet up to the seat, hugging my knees to my chest, and sighed. "Is it that obvious?"

"Uh, yeah. It really is."

After Max had left the hotel room, I told her the whole story so she knew nothing had happened. Well, nothing much, anyway. Just enough to make it a recurring topic of conversation, mostly with Krystal saying I should have gone for it all that night.

"Listen," she said, "if you're going to make your life here, you're going to have to get used to this sort of thing. Especially since you're going to be working around actors, directors, producers… I mean, think about it. You're pretty, single, and guys like you. This isn't Ohio, and it certainly isn't our little Podunk town."

She had a point. I was in uncharted waters and possibly in over my head. But if I was going to make it here, I'd have to learn to deal with it. That didn't mean I had to sleep with every guy who hit on me; it simply meant I'd have to become skillful at choosing the right ones to say yes to, and not leading on the ones I knew I'd say no to.

I shouldn't have led Max on like I did, and I felt a little guilty about that.

But the bigger immediate issue—in fact, the *biggest* issue—was what impact the other night would have on my work.

"Shit. What am I going to do if he turns down Jacqueline for the role and Kevin finds out why? I'll be screwed."

Krystal got up from the couch and grabbed her empty glass. She walked into the kitchen while answering. "I don't think there's anything you can do about that now. Except maybe call him up and sleep with him now."

"Come on, I'm serious."

"I know," she said, her voice carrying in from the kitchen. "Sorry. I wish I knew what to tell you. Do you want some wine?"

"Ugh. No, I've had plenty this weekend."

Krystal obviously wasn't going to be of much help, but I was hoping she'd have some insight for me. Even something small and seemingly insignificant that might spark a solution in my mind. But all hope was dashed when she came back into the room.

"Oh! The show's back on." She grabbed the remote and un-muted the television. "Sorry, I have to see what happens here."

I arrived at work Monday morning determined to get back in the mindset I was in before the Vegas trip, which meant focusing on work and only work, and that's what I did all week. Work during the day, Netflix at night.

We didn't hear from Max or his people all week. I talked to Jacqueline several times, and she was becoming increasingly difficult to deal with. She was convinced she wasn't going to get the part. Once again, I had to play therapist and keep her on an even keel.

Friday brought some comic relief in the form of an aspiring actor and complete jackass I had to meet with. Part of my job was doing preliminary reviews of unsolicited letters and resumes sent to us by people looking for an agent.

Sam Ryan arrived fifteen minutes late for the meeting, a bad first impression for an actor seeking representation. He wore black jeans, a white t-shirt, black leather jacket, and way too much aftershave.

We went to the conference room and started off with some small talk about the great weather and the horrible traffic, typical LA conversation pieces.

Within ten minutes, I knew I was dealing with a guy who thought too much of himself. He kept telling me how much casting directors didn't know what they were doing, how there's so much untapped talent out there and he was the "cream of the untapped crop," and how the industry was overly concerned with money to the detriment of art.

He was going nowhere with that attitude, and it wasn't my job to change him. He wouldn't have a chance in a meeting with Kevin.

His big mistake was telling me he'd been in two episodes of *Friends*, with speaking parts in both. He claimed he was supposed to have been a recurring character—an ex-boyfriend of Monica's. All of that would have been easy to check but I didn't have to. I was a huge fan of the show and I'd probably seen every episode three times. I would have remembered this guy. So I added "liar" to the list of negatives.

"So why aren't you repped now?" I asked.

"Well, my agent recently passed away, so that's why I'm looking."

I felt bad for asking the question with such a sarcastic tone. "Oh, I'm sorry to hear that. What was his name? Or her name?" I started shuffling through his still shots to find his resume.

"Estelle Leonard."

I stopped. That was the name of the agent who represented Joey's character on *Friends*. What the hell was with this guy? He was either abnormally stupid, or he thought I was. It was at this point that I decided he was no longer entertaining and I didn't have the patience to listen to any more of his bullshit.

I ended the meeting by standing and telling him, "Thanks for coming by. We'll be in touch." It was a nice way of saying *Don't call us, we'll call you*.

"You got plans tonight?" he asked.

I was stunned, considering how coldly I had treated him. "Excuse me?"

"I was just wondering if, you know, maybe we could 'hook up'," he said, using air-quotes.

"I really don't think so."

He lowered his voice, not for the benefit of privacy, but in an apparent attempt to sound sexy. "You don't know what you're missing out on."

"I have a boyfriend."

"So?"

"So, again, it's a no."

He stepped toward me, looking right at my chest. "You're really hot. Just tell me what it'll take."

Exasperated, I told him the truth. "You want to know what it will take? A serious lapse of judgment on my part." I stepped toward the conference room door, opened it, and stepped aside. I motioned out the door with my hand. "Good luck, Mr. Ryan."

He straightened up and started moving toward the door. I gave him a little more room.

"You don't have to be such a bitch about it," he said.

I let him get out of the room, almost all the way across the lobby, and when he reached for the main doors I said, "And *you* don't have to wear so much cheap aftershave!"

He kept going without looking back.

Kevin's office door opened and he poked his head out. "Everything okay?"

"Yeah, sorry. Everything's fine."

"Okay. I'm on a call, but give me..." He looked at his watch. "Give me about fifteen minutes and we'll go over some of those demo DVDs."

I was gathering the stuff off the conference room table to throw in the trash, wondering if Sam Ryan had been right. I had never thought of myself as a bitch before, but I guess it was inside me somewhere and all it took was a little stress and an annoying person to release it.

I was worried about the whole thing with Max and the impact my rejection would have on my job. Jesus. How stupid had I been, letting things get as far as they had? Kevin would probably fire me on the spot if he found out.

Back out in the open office area, I heard Kevin's door open. I looked in that direction and saw him waving me into his office. I put the package down on a desk and went in, where he motioned to me to have a seat, then put a finger up to his lips, telling me to be silent and just listen.

Kevin switched the phone to speaker and the room was filled with the smooth voice of Max Dalton.

Oh, shit. This is it, I thought. Max was going to tell Kevin that he decided to take a pass on Jacqueline Mathers. Then we'd lose her as a client. Kevin would probably find out what happened in Vegas, I'd lose my job, and I'd become the latest person to hear the proverbial "You'll never work in this town again" phrase. *Damnit, stomach, stop churning....* I felt like I was going to be sick right there on the floor in Kevin's office.

What I heard Max saying was: "...lots of auditions, live and on DVD, and this was one of the harder decisions I've had to make. Jacqueline is good. She's great looking and she's an absolute natural. Her lack of experience bothers me a little..."

Here it comes, I thought.

"...but it's not something that can't be overcome," Max was saying. Then he mentioned the director. "Gary and I talked it over, and he's equally impressed. We'd like to offer her the role."

Kevin gave a thumbs-up. "That's great to hear, Max."

I might have been even more thankful to hear the news than Kevin was. An incredible rush of relief washed over me and every muscle in my body relaxed. I hadn't ruined

Jacqueline's chances, or Kevin's business, or my own future. Now I could relax.

Max said, "I have the contract all ready to be signed. Maybe you can send over your assistant to pick it up."

So much for relaxing.

Kevin looked at me. "Uh, sure. No problem."

Keep breathing, I told myself. Great. I was now going to be in Max's office. Just when I thought all the worry and stress was over and done with.

"I'll be here for another hour or two."

"She'll be right over. And thanks again, Max. Look forward to working with you."

"Talk to you soon." *Click.*

Kevin tapped the screen on his phone and put it on the desk. "Do you have any idea how huge this is?"

"It's…yeah, just amazing." My voice lacked enthusiasm, but he didn't pick up on it.

"This is my biggest and most important deal so far." He stood and started pacing, walking off some nervous energy, I supposed. "But you already knew that." He looked at his watch. "You remember how to get to the studio, right? To Max's office?"

My stomach started churning again. "Yeah. Pretty sure."

Kevin reminded me about giving his name at the guard gate, and within five minutes I was in my car, navigating LA traffic, my mind racing with thoughts of seeing Max again.

FIVE

During the drive over to the studio, it struck me that maybe Max had given Jacqueline the part just to get me over to his office. Was that even possible?

No, surely it wasn't. My paranoia was getting the best of me. There was no way a big-shot Hollywood producer would hire an actress just to get some alone time with the assistant to the agent who repped the actress. Too much money at risk. His entire reputation could fall along with one flop movie.

It was ridiculous to think all of this was a ruse to get me over to his office. He had dozens of ways of doing that. Maybe not this immediately, but he could have accomplished it if he'd wanted to.

I got to the guard gate and was told where to park. As I walked across the lot, my eyes scanned my surroundings for famous people. Yes, I was still new enough to Hollywood to be star-gazing.

I found Max's office with no trouble. When I walked in, I was greeted by a tall blonde, and was struck by the very real possibility that she was the same woman Max was talking to that last morning in Las Vegas. I hadn't seen her face, but it made sense that his assistant might be there. Maybe she traveled with him all the time. Maybe she was there on her own and they just happened to run into each other. Or maybe he was fucking her....

Whatever the case, I hadn't met her the first time I was here.

She noticed me and said, "Hi, can I help you?"

"I'm Olivia Rowland. Here to see Max—Mr. Dalton."

"Oh, yes, he's expecting you. Go right on in." She gave me a friendly smile.

Max's reception area was larger than our entire office and it seemed like my heels were clicking extra loud as I made my way to the frosted-glass doors that led to his office. I took a deep breath, turned the handle, and stepped in.

Max was sitting on a couch just below a huge poster of the last movie he'd made. I'd been so nervous last time I was here, I hadn't noticed the details of his office. There was a large glass and chrome desk, a large black leather chair behind it, and two smaller versions on the other side. The walls held other movie posters—all large, expensively framed, and each had its own lighting.

"Olivia," he said, standing to greet me.

"Hi, Max."

"Please, come have a seat." He pointed at the couch.

I wanted to sit in one of the chairs opposite the couch, with the large coffee table separating us. Every move he made exuded confidence, grace, and sex. I knew I shouldn't sit next to him.

He held out his hand, inviting me, and I took it. But I sat several feet away from him.

Max lifted up his arm and took a dramatic sniff. "Do I smell bad?"

"No." *Actually you smell amazing*, I thought. "Why?"

"Because you sat so far away from me. I figured you had a good reason."

Did I ever. But I couldn't exactly tell him that I needed some space between us so I wouldn't get sucked into a replay of the other night in the hotel room.

I kept my voice level and professional. "I'm just here to pick up the contract."

Max slid down the couch until he was right next to me. I got a close-up look again at those deep eyes, and his perfectly shaped lips.

He put a finger under my chin. "I couldn't wait for you to get here." He leaned forward and kissed me—a soft kiss, no tongue.

When he pulled back I said, "We really need to stop this. Or…at least talk about it."

"Why ruin it with talking?"

Was he serious? He seemed to have a smooth way with women in all aspects, so why the hell would he even hint that talking wasn't necessary?

"Don't you think this is a bad idea?" I asked.

His eyes left mine, and his gaze drifted down my body—to my chest, then my legs, which were shown off by the skirt I wore. "I can't think of a better idea than you and me together."

"And by 'together' you mean sex, right? Just sex."

He shrugged. "Whatever you like. What *do* you like, Olivia?"

I'd never had such a blunt discussion like this before. It was making me a little nervous, but not to the point where I was going to lose my resolve. I did ask for something to drink, though, and Max immediately offered me a White Russian.

"Is that all you drink?" I asked.

He nodded as he stood and made his way to the bar area of his office. "Ever since high school. I never liked beer. Didn't like any of the other stuff I tried, either. But the White Russian…I fell in love with it from the start and I've been faithful ever since."

That got a laugh out of me. "I'll have a water, thanks."

"Sparkling or spring?"

"Just plain water. Whatever you've got."

I watched him standing at the bar, his back to me. Today he was wearing a long-sleeved, white t-shirt, blue jeans, and dark brown boots. The t-shirt clung to his torso, nicely showing off those wide shoulders and back, down to his trim waist. His semi-long brown locks curled right where the shirt collar started. I got to check out his nice ass for the first time, thanks to the jeans, and had to tear my eyes away from him before he turned around and caught me. It was as though he'd been carefully built, painstakingly constructed by someone with great taste and a serious attention to detail.

I looked out the large windows and for the first time saw the view he had of the studio lot. From his third-floor office, I could see several outdoor sets, some of which looked familiar from movies I'd seen. Far off in the distance, Hollywood's hills provided the backdrop. The only flaw in this view was not being able to see the famous sign on the hillside.

Max was making his drink as he said, "Just plain water, huh? I never figured you for a girl who likes anything plain."

"I don't like complications."

"Ah, that's too bad. Sometimes complications can be quite exciting. At least, that's what I've found."

Clearly, we were not talking about water here, and both of us knew it.

He joined me on the couch, handing me a bottle of plain water.

"So," he said, "you want to talk. Let's talk."

I sipped the cool water, trying to figure out what I was going to say.

"I'll go first," he said, saving me. "Let's just get this out in the open. We're attracted to each other. We're both single—"

"Are we?" I interrupted.

"I certainly am. Have I misjudged your situation?"

I shook my head. "No, you haven't."

"Good. So what's stopping you?"

I put the water bottle on the table and crossed my legs. "I don't do…this. I don't just randomly hook up with guys just because they're hot."

Max's face was taken over by a smile. "So you think I'm hot."

My head dropped. "Yes. Yes, I think you're hot, okay? Happy?"

He sipped his White Russian. "Happy? Yeah. I could be happier, though."

"Listen, what I'm saying is that it's going to take more than a few scripted lines and smooth moves to get in my pants."

"Actually, you're wearing a skirt. But that's just a technicality."

I liked his sense of humor and I couldn't help but laugh.

"And, for the record," he continued, "I haven't scripted any lines for this."

"Okay, I'll take your word for it."

He settled back on the couch more, closer to me. I smelled his wonderful manly scent again and almost asked him what he was wearing, but decided not to.

Instead, I said, "I'm not interested in a casting couch romp."

He threw his head back and laughed. When he looked back at me he said, "Neither am I, Olivia. In fact, I haven't heard of a casting couch 'romp' as you put it in my entire career in this town."

"No?"

He shook his head. "It's a thing of the past. At least, I think it is."

"You have your choice of women, I'm sure. Speaking of which, when I was leaving Las Vegas Sunday morning, I saw you with a blonde woman just outside the restaurant."

He cocked his head to the side. "Ah, yes. She was trying to sell me something."

"Yeah, I'll bet she was." I reached for my water bottle.

"She wasn't a prostitute. She works for the corporation that owns that hotel and casino and another one down the strip. She was trying to get me to buy another penthouse."

"*Another*?"

He nodded. "I have one in the hotel where we were."

Jesus. If he'd brought me up to his penthouse, I wouldn't have made it out of there without giving him what he wanted. I was close enough that night to wanting it that it would have been damn near a sure thing.

"So," I said, "are you going to get another one?"

Max frowned. "I can't see needing two in Vegas."

"Good point."

"Thank you." He smirked and sipped his drink. "Let's get back to the casting couch…"

"Let's not. What I need to get back to is work."

It would have been the perfect time to stand up, ask for the contract, and be on my way. But Max's hand was suddenly resting on my leg. I looked down and saw him turn his hand over, palm up, and he rubbed my knee with the back of his index finger.

I watched him do that for a few seconds, marveling at how that slight touch sent a shock of excitement up my leg. My chest felt heavy, and I felt my nipples puckering.

"You want this as much as I do," he said. "I see it in the way you look at me."

I turned my head to look at him and in a flash his face met mine, his lips taking mine. My mouth opened and his tongue took the invitation without hesitation. There was no stopping him, and at that point, I didn't have any desire to stop anything he was doing.

He controlled the kiss, heated and slick, taking the lead with his sensual licks along my tongue.

Max pulled away from my face for a moment. "You're not saying no."

"I haven't said yes, either."

"Let me try to make you say it."

His mouth took mine again.

Max's hand slid up my thigh slowly. My heart rate increased in anticipation. One finger slipped under the elastic of the leg hole in my panties, and I felt the tip of his fingers brush against my wet folds.

"Oh, God," I said into his mouth.

"That's almost a yes."

He kept teasing me with the tip of his finger, softly going a little farther each time, but not near my clit.

I took a handful of his hair and squeezed. It was thick, yet soft, and my grabbing it seemed to stir even more passion in him.

"We don't need to take this off," he said, tugging my shirt up. "But I have to see these."

Max unclasped my bra, pushing it aside, exposing my breasts.

"God, Olivia…" His voice trailed off as he lowered his head and sealed his lips around my nipple. I watched the tip of his tongue tweaking it, as his hand squeezed and plumped up my other breast.

He took the other nipple into his mouth. They were both getting tighter now, due to his attention, and also as the cool air rushed across the wetness he left behind.

My skirt was riding up my hips. Max hooked his thumb into the waistband of my panties and started pulling them down my legs.

I looked down and saw that they'd come off one leg, but were now dangling from my other ankle. Max guided that leg up to the arm of the couch, pulling my other one over his lap, and I was spread wide and open for him.

I'd never felt so vulnerable to a man before. But then I'd never been with a man who took control like this, either.

"You haven't said yes yet, Olivia."

"Isn't this position enough?"

He grinned. "Say it."

His hand had crept back up my thigh. His fingers curled around the underside, leaving his thumb hovering just over me.

I looked at him. "Yes."

I tilted my head back against the couch in reaction to his thumb making contact with my clit. He massaged it in slow circles, giving it more pressure, then less, then more again.

I was looking straight up at the ceiling when I felt his mouth on my neck. His tongue traced little circles, and then he'd suck a little.

The way he was working my clit was perfect, and I could have come just like that, but it wasn't enough for Max. He moved his hand and slipped one finger inside me, turning it as he let it slide in and out in short strokes.

"You're so open to me," he said.

That voice had been enough to get me wet before, but the effect was a thousandfold with his fingers in motion on me, and *in* me.

"God, Olivia, you're more than I bargained for."

I was thinking the same thing about him. My mind was focusing on his hand, though, as he slipped a second finger in.

"Oh, yes, please," I said.

"Tell me what you like."

"That. Right..th-th-there....oh, God...."

With my leg over his lap, I could feel his hard cock through his pants. I wanted to touch it. I wanted to make him feel as good as he was making me feel.

My hips bucked to meet his stroking fingers. I was holding nothing back.

I looked at Max. He was looking down between my legs so I looked down, too. If my legs had been spread any wider, they would have been perilously close to the cramping point. But there was no pain. It was all pleasure coming from Max's skilled hand.

The way he fingered me was better than any sex I'd ever had.

My breath hitched in my throat and I gasped.

I wondered if the door was locked, and then thought that if someone walked in I wouldn't have cared. This was too damn good.

I started moving the leg that was draped over his lap. Max's cock strained against his jeans. I don't know how he maintained the self-control to keep it there—he could have had his pants down in seconds and fucked me.

"I'm going to make you come, Olivia. This is all about you."

There was my answer as to why he kept his pants on. *This is all about you*. I'd never had a guy say that to me. Such an idea had probably never crossed the minds of the guys I'd been with.

"Are you ready to come for me?"

"Yes. Yes."

His mouth pressed to mine, deliciously powerful and possessive. He lowered his head and flattened his tongue over my nipple, then took it between his tongue and his upper teeth—a sensation of softness combined with just the slightest sharp edge.

His fingers picked up the pace, and the flat of his palm pressed against my clit. Perfect.

Max said, "You see how hot it could be? You and me?"

I was at the point where verbal responses were nearly impossible. At least coherent ones were. I made some kind of noise that was close to a squeak. Where did that come from? Max had drawn it out of me, somehow.

"Our sex will be so good. I could make you come a hundred different ways."

After this performance—was he auditioning?—I didn't doubt that he could.

"I want to see your eyes when you come, Olivia."

I'd had my head tilted back again, and when I moved and looked at him, his mouth was slightly open.

"You feel how hard you got me?"

I nodded, pressing my leg down and feeling his erection. I had an image of it ripping right through his jeans.

"It's going to be inside you soon, and you'll return the pleasure I'm giving you now."

"Max. Please....I want to...."

"Want to what? Want to come? Want to make me come?"

"All—all of it," I stammered.

A wicked smile grew on the edges of his mouth. "Not yet. Not all of it. This is all you right now."

"Oh, God, yes. I'm gonna..."

My words trailed off as he brought me to orgasm. My hips thrust against his hand. His two fingers were right on the spot I always found with my own fingers. A spot most guys never found, but Max had zeroed in on it with seemingly no effort.

"Look at me," he said.

I did what he said, and his eyes had the look of someone who'd just completed a major conquest.

He knew he had me. He knew I'd given in. It was the most turned-on I'd ever been and I hadn't held back one bit. There was an intensity to making myself vulnerable to him that I hadn't expected. It was easier than I'd thought it would have been, and the payoff was beyond my wildest expectation.

Max's face was close to mine, so close that our foreheads were touching. He looked deep into my eyes as the fog of the orgasm lifted from me and I slowly faded back into reality.

Max was hooking my bra again, and pulling my shirt back down to cover me. He moved off the couch and knelt on the floor, lifted the ankle that still held onto my panties, and looped them over my other ankle. I moved my hips to accommodate him as he pulled them up my legs to my waist. After straightening my skirt, he sat beside me once again.

I was thinking how unique it was that he made sure I was dressed again, covered, and not having to feel uncomfortable after the moment for vulnerability had passed.

"Thank you," I said.

He kissed my forehead, then my cheek, and then gave me a long, slow, sweet kiss on the lips.

I wanted to stay, but I needed to go. "I have to get back to work."

"Right. Wouldn't want Kevin to wonder what was going on." He smiled. "I'll get the contract."

I went and stood by his office doors while he got the envelope. When he handed it to me, I started to take it, but he held on and tugged on it.

I looked up at him. He had a playful smile on his face.

"Thanks for coming to get this, Ms. Rowland."

"It was nice to see you again, Mr. Dalton."

He let go of the large envelope. I held it close to my chest. I was waiting for a goodbye, maybe a little peck of a kiss on the cheek. Instead, he leaned in, kissed my ear and said, "Next time we won't be rushed, and I'm going to take my time fucking you."

I swallowed hard. The bluntness in his tone was shocking, and almost surely would have made me laugh if it had come out of any other man's mouth. But the truth is, I was aroused by it.

He reached for the door handle, but before he opened it I said, "When exactly is next time?"

Damnit. There was a note of desperation in my question that I hadn't intended to be there.

He looked up as though he were trying to find the answer. "I think I'll let it be a surprise."

SIX

“That sure took a long time,” Kevin said as I walked into the office.

“Sorry.”

I tried not to make eye contact with him, even though I knew it would only make it seem even more like I was hiding something.

“Well?” he said. “What happened?”

“With what?”

“Are you okay?”

“I’m fine. Why?”

He squinted a little and looked at me sideways. “You don’t look okay. You look…different. Is something wrong?”

I’d heard of “just-fucked hair” before but was there such a thing as “just-finger-fucked hair”? Was that what he was referring to? Or maybe I was just so nervous about being found out that it showed on my face. Either way, I didn’t want him to elaborate.

“Everything’s fine, Kevin. I got the contract.” I reached into my bag to get the envelope. “And then after I left, I needed to stop somewhere and take care of something.”

He looked like he didn’t believe me.

I lowered my voice and added, "Personal stuff." I made a kind of embarrassed looking face for effect, and it appeared as though he bought the story.

"Ah, sorry," he said.

I shook my head. "No worries." I handed the envelope to Kevin.

He opened it, took out the contract and quickly scanned it. "Do you have any idea what these papers mean? This is huge for me." He looked at it again with extreme pride on his face.

"I'm so happy for you."

He looked up from the papers. "Happy for *us*. You're part of the team here. I couldn't have done this without your help."

It saddened me to hear that. For one thing, it was a humble thing for him to say, and that wasn't something you came across very often in Hollywood. And secondly, while I knew it was true that I'd done a lot to help him land the role for Jacqueline, I'd also done a lot to put Kevin's business in jeopardy.

All it would take is one rumor about Kevin using young assistants to persuade studio execs in a less than ethical manner.

I couldn't have been happier that it was Friday and I had two full days to be away from Kevin and the office.

All I could think about for the rest of the day was when I'd see Max again. He said he'd let it be a surprise, and when I was leaving his office I thought it sounded exciting. But by the end of the workday it was just nerve-wracking.

I had plans that night to go to a club with Krystal and two of her friends I'd recently met. Maybe that would serve as a good distraction from all things Max.

"This dress makes me look like a whore, doesn't it?"

I was in my bathroom putting on makeup when Krystal walked in and asked the question. I remembered her asking me that when we were in Vegas. I looked at her in the mirror. She had on a tight, peach-colored strapless dress that went all the way down to her feet. It was gorgeous on her, but I wondered what would happen if she accidentally stepped on the hem. There was no way her boobs wouldn't pop out if that happened.

"Why do you keep asking me if you look like a whore?"

She turned to the side and looked at her profile in the mirror. "I don't know. I just don't want to look like a cheap skank."

"You look great. Just one thing, though..." I told her about the hem and she said she'd already thought of that, and if it happened, maybe it would be the highlight of the night.

"That would be an understatement," I said.

I finished getting ready, all the while debating whether or not to tell her about what had happened in Max's office earlier in the day. Frankly, I was amazed by my restraint.

Krystal gave directions as I drove us to her favorite club, a place called Drais located atop the W Hotel on Hollywood Boulevard. Having been to Las Vegas, I was somewhat ready for the action—the lights, music, well-dressed and good-looking people—but this was a step up. These were Hollywood's hottest hanging out in a place that was a restaurant, pool, and nightclub. Inside, the music was loud, lighting showcased the red, black, purple, and green walls. Big comfortable chairs and couches were everywhere. People were dancing beneath oversized floor lamps, complete with shades. Even more people were out by the pool.

It was a gorgeous night. From the vantage point of the rooftop of the W Hotel, I had a completely new perspective on LA. At least I did in a visual sense.

We found two of Krystal's friends who she'd been meaning to introduce to me—Julia and Rachel. They were also aspiring actresses, and within ten minutes of being introduced to them I heard them talk more about auditions and agents than Krystal had in the month I'd been living with her. Odd.

When they got around to talking about the famous people they had seen here before, Max's name came up.

"Speak of the devil," Julia said.

We all looked in the direction she nodded toward.

Holy shit. There he was. Over by the outdoor bar area. He was speaking to two men I didn't recognize, and then we made eye contact. A slow grin appeared on his face and he mouthed the word: "Surprise."

And surprised I was. Actually, that's not even the word for it. There might not be a good one to describe what I felt—my breath hitched in my throat, my knees got weak, and I felt a tingling sensation all over my skin that left my nipples hard and a faint ache between my legs.

"I've heard stories about that guy," Julia said.

Krystal looked at me with a worried expression. I was glad I hadn't told her what had happened in Max's office earlier that afternoon.

Rachel sipped her margarita. "Do tell."

Yes, please do tell, I thought. Maybe I needed to know more about Max before I let him give me the surprise he'd promised earlier.

"Total womanizer," Julia said.

Krystal looked at me, then at Julia. "Have you been on the receiving end of it?"

Julia said, "No, but I've heard things. Lots of things."

"Like what?" I asked.

"Just that he's fucked a lot of actresses."

Krystal laughed. "Oh, the horror. Hey, it's Hollywood. He's hot and single. No laws against him doing what he wants."

Julia turned to Krystal. "Don't tell me you—"

"Nope." Krystal shook her head. "I've only seen him in person one time, actually." She looked at me.

"You?" Julia said, giving me a look up and down, like I was someone Max wouldn't look twice at. At least that's how I took it.

I didn't bother to answer her. I just smiled. I knew what was about to happen, and I decided to let that speak for itself.

Rachel swirled her drink. "He could do whatever he wants with me. Look at that body. Damn." She was biting her lower lip.

"Oh, holy shit." Julia's eyes got huge. "Is he… Yep. He's coming over here."

"Come to mama," Rachel purred.

But he didn't go to Rachel. He came up to me.

"Hello, Olivia." He kissed my cheek.

I whispered, "What are you doing here?"

His mouth was still near my ear. "Surprise…"

Rachel and Julia looked at me, shock registering on their faces. They looked at Krystal, who shrugged, with a grin on her face.

Max put his hand on the small of my back. "Everyone having a good time so far?"

Krystal and the girls said they were.

I didn't bother introducing him to Rachel and Julia. Their disdain for me was obvious in the way they looked at me, but I didn't care.

Max looked at me, then at the girls. "I hope you ladies don't mind, but I need to steal Olivia away for a little while."

All three shook their heads.

When we got a few feet away, Max asked me who drove.

"I did. Why?"

"You should give your car key to Krystal."

"Why?"

"So she can get home."

I laughed nervously. "I know what you meant, but...where are we going?"

He kissed me lightly on the lips. "It's a surprise, remember?"

I got my car key out of my bag and walked the few steps back to Krystal and handed her the key.

"You're leaving?"

I shrugged. "I don't know."

Julia and Rachel both looked at me with their mouths open.

"He said he has a surprise for me," I said. "I'll see you later. Or tomorrow. Or...whenever."

I turned on my heel and walked away, feeling like I'd just won the championship round of the catty girl playoffs.

SEVEN

Thirty minutes later, we were in Malibu, turning into the driveway of a huge house. Palm trees dotted the lawn, and the house was illuminated by lights shining up from the ground.

Max pulled into the garage, turned off the car and said, "I can't wait to get you into my house." He got out and came around to open my door for me. When I stood, he took me in his arms and kissed me ferociously.

"I can't wait to see your house. It looks beautiful."

"That's not why I want you inside." He took my hand and led me inside.

We entered through a door in the garage, and it led right into an expansive living room. It was dark—everything from the walls to the floor to the furniture, shades of rich browns and reds, with small pools of light from lamps around the room. His office was bright and modern looking, but his home was all warm tones, very masculine.

Just like him. And just like the possessive way he kissed me again when we were barely inside the house.

My purse dropped to the floor. Max slid the zipper down the back of my dress and it fell to my ankles. I stepped out of it, finding myself standing there in my bra, panties, and heels.

"You have a way of getting me naked, Max."

"I love when you're exposed to me."

His lips sealed around mine, his tongue hungrily exploring my mouth.

I managed to pull away a little. "Don't I get to see you?"

He moaned from deep in his chest. "I want you to see me. Undress me."

His hands fell to his sides and he stood before me, waiting.

Holy shit. I was about to undress Max Dalton and see his gorgeous self in the nude.

I untucked his shirt and slid it up his body, my hands underneath, feeling the muscles in his stomach and chest. I unbuttoned his shirt, pulled it over his shoulders and it joined my clothes on the floor.

He was in just as good a shape as I'd imagined. His chest was broad, covered by a thin field of fine hair. I put my hands on his pecks and felt how taut they were.

When I looked up at Max's face, I saw his eyes smoldering with intensity. I kept eye contact with him as I lowered my hands down his stomach and found his belt. Hearing the metal-on-metal *clink* as I unfastened the buckle was like a chiming alert: *You're about to touch his cock…*

And that's what I did. My hand slipped beneath the waistband of his boxers and before I knew it my fingers were touching the base of his erection. I moved my hand to wrap it around his girth, and felt how thick he was.

Max's hands came up to the sides of my face, and he pulled me to his mouth. A searing hot kiss followed as my hand explored his length. The skin was velvety soft, sheathing the hardest and biggest cock I'd ever felt. A rush of excitement burst through me as I thought about how I was the object of his driving desire.

"God, Olivia, your touch is so perfect."

He kissed me again as he unhooked my bra. My breasts felt heavy and he took each of them in his hands, cupping them, rubbing my nipples with his thumbs.

I kissed his neck and down his chest and stomach, lowering myself to my knees. I unzipped his pants and pulled them down along with his boxers. My first look at his cock. It was long and thick, sticking straight out and twitching with eagerness. It seemed like I looked at it for several minutes, but I know it was only seconds. Just as I was about to take him into my mouth he touched my shoulder and urged me to stand.

Max wrapped his hands around my waist. "I want you on the couch." He lifted me with ease and took the few steps toward the couch, setting me down on my back.

"I've wanted to taste you all day," he said, kissing down my neck, my chest, stopping at each nipple and tracing rings around them with his tongue. They hardened into tight peaks under his movements.

Max was kneeling on the floor as I lay sort of sidelong on the couch. He pulled my underwear down my legs swiftly, almost yanking them, and at that moment I wouldn't have cared if he'd torn them off of me.

He raised my legs with one of his large, strong hands holding my ankles together, and removed my heels.

He licked the backs of each calf, then down behind my knees, where it almost tickled a little, but this was too hot an experience for tickling. Down my thighs, kissing, sucking…staying there, sucking…

Was he giving me a hickey on the back of my thigh? Marking me? *Whoa.*

When he parted my legs, he guided one to drape over his shoulder. He pushed the other out, far, spreading me wide open just as he'd done on the couch in his office.

"I love it when you're so open for me," he said, echoing my thoughts.

"Max..." My voice trailed off. I couldn't get any words out. I'm not even sure what I would have said, anyway.

He kissed the inside of each thigh, lingering a little on the second one, opening his mouth and letting his teeth drag along my skin. Then buried his face between my legs, his tongue fluttering along my wet flesh.

Max used his fingers to part me, exposing my overly excited clit to him. When his tongue made first contact with it, I wanted to stay like that for a while, maybe hours, maybe days...I just didn't want him to stop.

My hips rolled along with his touch—his tongue making circular movements around my clit, my body making movements in the opposite direction, creating a friction like none other I'd ever felt. My body was begging for it and Max was giving me all I could handle.

I was insanely turned on by the noises he made—moaning and almost growling in his own pleasure, pleasure he was deriving from pleasing me.

"Max, I'm so close..."

I felt his hot breath on me as he spoke between licks. "Come for me. Come in my mouth."

"Don't stop."

I writhed along with his tongue strokes, the orgasm jolting through me. My stomach muscles flexed, relaxed, repeated, and my body shook as I threw my head back into the pillow and cried out his name.

He moaned, adding a vibration to the licking, and the orgasm intensified as it rocked through every inch of my body.

As the orgasm was subsiding, Max stayed where he was, kissing my inner thighs. After a moment, he moved up over me, his mouth immediately going to mine. I felt the hunger in his kiss—deep, passionate, wanting, *needing.*

He knelt between my legs and ripped open the foil packet holding the condom. I watched as he rolled it down his magnificent length. I could hear my heart beating in my ears. I wanted more. I needed more.

My head rolled to one side when he put his hand beside it on the couch. The weight of him and the forcefulness with which he moved causing the cushion to give way. My arms were just over my head. Max grabbed them both with one hand, holding my wrists together like he'd done with my ankles, pinning me in place on the couch.

I watched his face. His lips pressed together, his nostrils flared, and his eyes were staring hard at me with lust. I was underneath a man who was intent on having me, owning me sexually, driving toward his own release.

"Ready, Olivia?"

I nodded.

"Good, because I was going to fuck you either way."

I felt the head of his cock notch between my folds. He pushed a little and I took the first inch or so.

"You're so tight."

"Uh huh..." The pitch of my voice was high again. Max had a way of making me sound unlike my usual self.

He pushed in all the way in one hard thrust, sending my head back into the pillow as my back and neck arched, taking all of him in. I felt his balls against me.

I gasped. Max was so hard, so big, so deep, I wasn't sure I could take any more without coming fast.

His mouth went to my neck and I felt his lips suck on my skin, then his tongue lapping at me as he said my name again and pulled back—almost all the way out, then drove back inside me with a long stroke.

I'd never been controlled like this during sex before, never had a man hold my wrists and possess me like this. I'd never even thought about it. There might have been an uncomfortable, even scary, aspect to it, but Max did it with great skill. Totally in control, and totally focused on our pleasure.

His hips rocked back and forth, then in an almost circular motion, as his cock filled me and touched every part of my swollen core.

"You feel so fucking good," he growled.

He lowered his head to my chest and took a nipple into his mouth. He sucked it in softly, but then pressed his lips together, teasing and pulling my nipple to its full hardness. Max looked at it, licked it, and then gave the same attention to the other one.

He let my hands go and he placed his hands on either side of me. I reached up and felt his upper arms flex. They held his weight as he fucked me harder. Max was almost fierce in his thrusts. His breathing was getting deeper and shorter.

He was stroking pleasure into me as he stroked himself to his own pleasure. I wanted him to get off on it and have the best orgasm he'd ever had.

He kissed me again, taking my tongue into his mouth and then sucking on it. The intensity of his fucking increased and I started making little noises into his mouth, which only made him move his hips with more force.

I felt his cock throbbing, pulsating, getting closer to coming. My hands were tightly clenching his upper arms and I felt his muscles grow tighter. I looked up and saw him tilt his head back. Then he faced me again, took my lips in a wild kiss and said, "I'm going to come inside you, Olivia."

I'd never been fucked like this before. Never had a man so determined to fuck me like this. Never had a guy talk to me so sweetly and so dirty at the same time. I'd never been turned on this much and it made me want to give Max whatever he wanted.

"Do you want it?" he breathed.

"Yes, come. I want you to come so bad."

It was hard to get the words out. He was taking my breath away, literally. I gasped and shook as I began to feel another orgasm rising within me from the point where Max's thick cock was rubbing against me in perfect rhythm.

"Fuck…" His voice was low and breathy.

I felt him tense up. His thrusts slowed almost to a stop. Then he plunged back into me, deep, and moved his hips vigorously as he pumped into the condom.

"Jesus, Olivia," he was saying as he came.

He lowered his body onto me and held me tight. I loved the weight of his body on mine, his exhaustion a result of his harsh lust for me.

We lay like that for a few moments, and then Max repositioned us both so that I was lying next to him on the big, wide couch, with my arms crossed on his chest and my head resting on them, looking at the face of this man who wanted me so badly.

EIGHT

We must have stayed there on the couch for about thirty minutes, basking the glow of what we'd just done.

"That was amazing," Max said.

"The best."

I wasn't lying. It was indeed the best sex I'd ever had, no doubt due to him being the hottest guy I'd ever been with, and the way he did it—taking control, taking *me.*

I didn't know what was going to come next. I really had no expectations, but what did end up happening was a shock.

"Are you ready?" he said.

I looked at him with a smile on my face. "That depends. I'm wiped out from what we just did." I laughed, and in a few seconds, I would regret it.

"You can rest on the way. I'll make sure you get inside okay."

What? He was taking me home. I didn't want to ask why, and feeling more than overwhelmed by the development, I probably wasn't in the right frame of mind to have the conversation. On top of that, what was I going to do? Beg him to let me stay there?

We barely spoke on the drive back to LA. The longer we were in the car, the more I felt hurt, used, and cheap. I wondered where my name would be on the roster of other women he'd brought home, fucked so passionately, and then dismissed.

When we got to my place he said, "I'll walk you to the door."

"No, you don't have to. Really." I gathered my purse and reached for the door handle.

"Olivia, hang on a second." He grabbed my hand and brought it to his face. He kissed the back of it and said, "Thank you for an incredible evening."

I produced the best fake smile I could and quickly got out of the car without saying anything. I made my way up the walkway, got to the door, put the key in the lock…all without turning around to look at him sitting there in his car. It took an amount of willpower I didn't know I possessed to do that.

I stepped inside and immediately went to the bathroom. I looked at myself in the mirror and the tears started flowing.

How could I have been so stupid? So gullible? Why had I let my guard down? Why had I let a man use and control me like that?Fuck! I knew better!

All the negative thoughts I used to have, after Chris, came thundering back into my mind. I blamed myself for everything that had happened that night, just as I'd blamed myself for letting myself become so vulnerable to Chris Cooper.

What Chris had done was a far cry from what Max had just done to me, but it was all about letting myself be vulnerable—something that's always fraught with danger, which is what makes it such a powerful act, but something I just wasn't ready to do again, and look what happened.

I got myself together emotionally and left the bathroom. Maybe Krystal was still up, and she'd let me vent my frustrations. There'd probably be a big "I told you so" to deal with, but at that moment I didn't care. I just didn't want to be alone.

When I got to her room, I found that she wasn't there.

Great. I was alone.

I thought of calling Grace, but it was getting close to one o'clock in the morning here in LA, so it was really late in Ohio. There was no way I could call her. Maybe it was for the best that I couldn't talk to my sister right now.

Physical and emotional exhaustion brought sleep. Quickly, thank God. I needed the rest.

What I didn't need, though, was the dream: *I'm standing with my back to the wall, and he has me trapped. He's backlit, and all I can see is his silhouette, standing about two feet in front of me. I have no escape. My body shakes with fear. Adrenaline is coursing through my veins. I could try to run, but I know he'd catch me. I see the silhouette's right shoulder dip and pull back. Then the most frightening thing I'd ever seen: he has made a fist and he's cocking his arm back for the punch, level with my face.*

I woke up, thankful that it was only a dream, that I hadn't been hit, and the only damage done was to my sheets as I lay there soaking in a cold sweat.

Damn Max. No, damn *me* for letting my guard down and letting another into my safety zone.

People say I have put up a wall after the incident with Chris. But what they don't know is that it's more than a wall. It's a fortress. There's a moat around it, and the water below is filled with alligators. There's a drawbridge with tripwires that will flare up with great bursts of fire if a man tries to cross it.

So how the hell had Max Dalton infiltrated the fortress?

I stripped the bed of the soaked sheets, and took off my clothes. I laid back down, naked, on the naked bed, and thankfully sleep came once again…this time without a dream.

When I woke in the morning, there was still no sign of Krystal, but my car was there. I'd been hoping she would let me unload on her.

I ended up not seeing her for the rest of the weekend. I texted her a few times, but got no response. I knew I couldn't call Grace and tell her everything. And when Sunday rolled around—the day I always called my parents and checked in—I didn't feel like talking to them. I sent an email instead, feigning a cold with a sore throat, and apologizing for not being able to talk. My dad wrote back within thirty minutes, relaying my mom's best home remedy for a sore throat. I felt bad for lying to them, but I just couldn't talk to them right then. I had no choice.

I spent the weekend alone, watching things I'd put in my Netflix queue.

In a way, I both dreaded and looked forward to Monday morning equally. I knew I couldn't skip work, no matter how badly I wanted to avoid looking like something was wrong and having Kevin ask me about it. The flipside of the coin was that I'd have something aside from streaming movies to focus on, and not think about how stupid I'd been to go that far with Max.

Kevin called shortly after I opened the office and told me he'd be out all day. I breathed a sigh of relief. I could ease back into my work for a day.

I finally got in touch with Krystal when eating my lunch salad at my desk.

"How was your weekend?" she asked.

"Okay."

"What happened with Max?"

The floodgates opened and I told her the whole story.

When I was finished she said, "What an ass! See, this is what I was telling you to be ready for."

"I know, I know." I didn't want a lecture.

"And he didn't call you all weekend?"

"Nope."

"Ah, forget him," she said. "I know you have a working relationship with him and all, but just keep it at that."

I didn't say anything.

Krystal said, "So…was it good?"

I sighed. "Best ever."

She chuckled. "Okay, so you just chalk it up as the best sex ever and move on. Gotta keep moving in this town."

"Speaking of which, what were *you* doing all weekend?"

"Oh, God. I met these two guys…" She went on to tell me the story of spending the weekend with two men, complete with the raunchy details of her first threesome.

"Are you fucking kidding me?" I said.

"Nope."

"Damn. And here I was thinking you were working and I just kept missing you or something." It wasn't really what I thought. How would I have missed her between shifts? I was starting to figure out that Krystal had some kind of wild and quite unique lifestyle. And I was starting to puzzle together that her lifestyle didn't involve working in a restaurant and going to auditions. But I didn't want to pry. Not yet, anyway.

We didn't talk any more about it for the rest of the week. I only saw her on Wednesday night, anyway, and just for a few minutes as I was heading off to bed when she got home.

I called my parents for a few minutes on Tuesday to let them know I was doing better, working, and everything else was going fine. Grace happened to be there when I called and we talked for a few minutes.

She lowered her voice at one point and said, "I ran into Chris at the gas station."

Hearing his name sent a shiver down my spine and brought back the imagery of the dream I'd had over the weekend.

"I don't even want to know."

"Well," she said, "he wanted to know about you."

"What did you tell him?"

There was a pause. Total silence.

"Grace? What did you tell him?" I asked, a stern tone in my words.

"I told him you moved to California."

"Uh huh. And?"

I heard a door close, and then it sounded like wind wooshing across the phone. She'd gone outside to get out of earshot of our parents.

"I'm sorry," she said. "I know it was stupid. I just wanted him to know that you were doing fine, and even better, without him. I wanted to make him feel like crap."

I gritted my teeth. "If he calls here—"

"He's not going to find out where you work. LA is huge, right?"

I leaned back in my chair. I didn't want to argue about this. "You still shouldn't have told him anything."

"I know. I'm sorry."

"But," I said, "I do want that asshole to know I'm not crushed without him. It's kind of my only sense of…victory or something, you know?"

We got past that little issue and she caught me up on the baby and other things going on in our little hometown. For the first time, and rather strangely, I felt a little tug of nostalgia. Not quite homesickness. Not yet, anyway. I figured it was simply an easy fantasy escape coping mechanism to deal with the fact that I hadn't really adjusted to the hustle and bustle of

LA and Hollywood yet. Kind of a yearning for the slower, simpler times.

NINE

There was nothing slow or simple about the way the rest of the week played out.

When I got home Wednesday after work, I found two dozen red roses on my doorstep, along with a card that said: *Sorry I've been so busy. Thinking of you and want to see you again soon. I'll call. – M*

My initial thought was gratitude that he'd had the sense not to send it to my office.

My second thought was how to tell him I just wasn't ready for something so intense, especially something fraught with so much possibility of letdowns.

I had come to the conclusion that I wasn't ready to date. Nor was I ready for a fuck buddy. And I really wasn't—and might never be—ready for a high-intensity relationship with someone like Max.

My self-esteem kept chiming in and telling me I wasn't pretty enough, rich enough, or sophisticated enough for someone like Max. The really depressing thing was that I felt like I was only good enough for someone like Chris Cooper. He'd done a real number on me, and while I had been able to break away from it for a while and enjoy the powerful seduction of Max, I was still drawn back to that self-defeating belief.

It seemed like a nearly impossible thing to admit to him, but there was a part of me that figured once he heard even half the story he would probably be gone in the blink of an eye.

So be it.

He called around 8 p.m. that night. I was putting some clothes in the washer when my phone rang. I looked at the caller ID and let it go to voicemail. I heard no voicemail alert, and then the phone rang again.

I took a deep breath and answered it.

He said, "Hey, babe."

Babe? I might have taken that as a cute term of endearment had the situation been different, and had I not talked myself into this frenzy of doubt over being his latest score.

"Max, I—"

"Before you say anything, I'm on the way over."

"What?"

"I'm about ten minutes away from your place. Thought I'd stop by."

"I wish you'd called before," I said.

"I just did, but you didn't answer."

"You know what I mean."

Screw it. I might not be ready for the talk, but it had to happen sooner or later. And since he was on his way over, it looked like this was going to happen sooner.

Ten minutes later, just as he'd promised, Max knocked on my door.

When I opened it, he somehow looked even better than he had before. Or maybe it was just my subconscious reminding me what I was about to do—tell this gorgeous, rich man to take a hike because I couldn't deal with the jealousy, distrust, and doubt.

He wore black slacks, with a blue button-down shirt. Simple. Understated. But damn, so sexy on him. He had one hand on the doorjamb, the other behind his back, striking a relaxed pose.

After our phone call, I had rushed into my room and changed out of my ratty sweatpants and t-shirt, back into the clothes I'd worn to work that day. It may seem kind of silly, trying to look my best and not wanting him to see me so casual, when this was going to be the last time we'd ever be around each other casually. From this point on, it would be all business. And that's why the professional attire worked.

"Ready for work?" he said, going for light-hearted.

I forced a smile. "We need to talk."

I moved aside and he stepped across the threshold. "Those are never good words."

As he moved past me, Max brought his hand around from behind his back and produced a bottle of wine. Great. He'd come here thinking that we'd have a few glasses of wine, loosen up, and have a roll in the sack.

"Your favorite," he said.

I looked at it for a second but made no move to take it.

"What's wrong, Olivia?"

I looked down at the floor. "Let's sit down."

He followed me into the den. I sat in a chair as Max took a seat on the couch. He put the bottle of wine on top of a magazine on the coffee table. "Not even going to sit beside me?"

"Max...I'm sorry. I can't do this."

"If it's a bad time—"

"No." I sighed, dropping my head into my hands. *Breathe, Olivia. Gather your strength and get this over with.* "I can't do this. Us. What we're doing. I'm sorry." My words were coming out in nearly incoherent sputtering.

"Is this about the other night?"

I nodded. "But not the sex. It was the brush-off."

"I wasn't brushing you off."

"Max, please. Let me finish."

"Sorry. Go on."

I took a slow, deep breath. "I shouldn't have let things go as far as they did. It was my fault. I should have trusted my instincts." I looked down at my hand as though examining my fingernails, then looked back up at him. "There's something you don't know about me. I have some...baggage, to put it mildly. Things that happened before I moved here. I'm not ready for a relationship, or dating, or any of this."

Max leaned back on the sofa and put his arms behind his head. "Tell me."

"I just told you."

"Tell me what happened," he pleaded.

"I don't want to go into it. The details aren't important."

He sat forward quickly, then got on the floor on one knee. It was too close to looking like a proposal.

"Don't," I said, sliding back on the chair.

He put his hand on my knee. "We all have baggage, Olivia. You think I took you home the other night for no reason?"

"What do you mean?"

"Baggage. I have it, too."

I looked at him through the tears that were welling up in my eyes. "Tell me."

He gave me a half-smile. "I asked first."

I laughed.

"I'll tell you," he said. "And I'll go first. I'll share with you if you share with me."

"Okay."

He sat on the floor, extended his long legs out, and leaned back on his hands. "I'm not going to lie; I've had my share of flings. All Hollywood cliché bullshit. All of it. Sometimes I wonder if there's a single person in this town who's real. I guess it shouldn't be surprising that everyone here is playing some part in their own little film of their life. Do you know how long it's been since I've had a meaningful conversation with a woman?"

I shook my head.

"Me either," he said. "I gave up trying to remember the last time. The worst part is, everyone's after something. A part in a movie. Money. Being seen on a red carpet. It doesn't matter what it is, if I have it, someone wants it, and there's no shortage of women who'll do anything to get it. I've played the game long enough. It's not interesting anymore. There's no challenge, no mystery, no romance."

"Wow."

He was speaking with such conviction, he almost looked pissed off about it.

"I'm not even doing what I love anymore," he said.

"Making movies? But you're at the top now."

He threw his head back, and I felt kind of silly, like I'd missed something. And I had.

"That's a whole different issue for another time. I shouldn't have brought it up."

"But I want to know," I said, getting on the floor next to him. God, I wanted to know. What was in the mind and heart of this man?

He shook his head. "It's not important right now. What *is* important is that now you know why I didn't let you get too close to me. Do you see this like I do? What we did was amazing. Mind-blowing, actually. But there's something more to having someone stay in your bed overnight."

"I do see it like that. But—"

"Wait. I know what you're going to say. You're not like the girls I just described. I know that now. Hell, I knew it then. But it's almost a reflex now. I shouldn't have done that. And I'm sorry I handled it like that with you."

We were silent for a moment. I wanted to kiss him, but more than that, I wanted him to kiss me. He didn't.

"Now," he said. "Unload your baggage. We had a deal."

"I know." I took a breath. "I had a relationship with a guy for three years, back in Ohio. I was headed down the same road as my mom and my sister—find a guy, get married, have kids. I found the guy, but it turned out he found other girls, too."

Max frowned.

"Three of them, to be exact," I said. "I found out about the first two at the same time. Before I got up the nerve to confront him, I found out about the third. That's when I told him I was done, it was over, so long, all that."

"It didn't go well," Max said, as if he already knew, but there was no way he could know. He just guessed there was a lot more.

I let out a deep sigh. "Not well at all. I'd never seen him so angry. I wasn't scared of him, but I didn't want to see him ever again. I stopped going out with my friends because I thought I'd run into him. I'd go to the mall and be nervous that he'd be there and we'd have an argument. He was calling me all the time, leaving messages, texting, pretty much begging me to forgive him. He came to our house one night—I was living at home—and my father had to call the police to get rid of him. It was getting that bad."

"Stalker."

"Yep. So, anyway, he shows up at my house one day when my parents aren't there. I'm at the kitchen table getting resumes and cover letters together. Regular day. And then he just walks in. Right into the kitchen, through the door that leads to the backyard."

Max sat forward, closer to me. "Jesus, Olivia."

I got a little choked up talking about it again. Max put his hand on my leg and gave it a light, comforting squeeze.

"So," I said, battling back the tears, "he's saying he just wants to talk and I'm telling him to leave. He refuses. I stand up and yell at him to leave, telling him I'm going to call the police. That's when he moved around the table before I could even process what was happening. He backed me up against the wall and said—I'll never forget these words—he said, 'I'll never let you love anyone else.' And I said, 'I don't love you.'"

Max's eyebrows rose. For a split second, I thought how surprising that was. Here was a writer, a story-teller, successful maker of movies, riveted by my story.

I needed to get the story over with. I hated thinking about it, much less talking about it. "That's when he raised his fist and cocked his arm back, like he was about to punch me in the face. God, the anger I saw in his eyes…it was terrifying. I'd never seen that in him before. I'd never seen that in *anyone*."

"Did he hit you, Olivia?"

I shook my head. "No. I just crumbled right there in front of him. Fell right to the floor, hysterically crying. I don't know if that's what stopped him or what. I just stayed on the floor and after a minute or so, I saw his shoes turn the other way and he left. Just walked out. Didn't say anything."

Max moved closer and put his arm around me.

I said, "You're only the second person I've told."

He lowered his head to my shoulder and kissed it. Then he looked up, put a finger under my chin and turned my face toward his. "I'm sorry, Olivia."

"It's not your fault."

"No, about how I handled the other night."

"Oh, well, that *is* your fault." I smiled.

Thankfully, Max had a sense of humor and took my sarcasm in stride.

We were silent for a few moments and then he had the best idea I'd heard in a long time.

"I'm not going to ask to stay here, or ask you to come home with me. I'm going to leave, and tomorrow I'll pick you up, we'll go on a date—a *real* date, our first one—and we'll make all of this right. Like it's all new. How does that sound?"

I threw my arms around his neck and pulled him close. "Perfect."

"Good. Are you okay after that talk? Okay to be by yourself?"

I nodded. "I'm fine."

We moved toward the door. While it was a little strange with him leaving after we'd opened up to each other on such a deeply personal level, it was also thrilling. The anticipation of a real date with Max Dalton was taking over the sadness of having to tell my story. Somehow, Max knew exactly the right thing for us to do next if we were going to move forward.

He stopped at the door, took me in his arms and kissed me sweetly.

"Just one thing," I said. "After what we did on your couch the other day, I'm not sure *everything* will be so new."

Max grinned to match my teasing facial expression. In the sexiest tone he said, "Oh, you just wait." And with that, he opened the door and left.

I wasn't sure I wanted to wait. I felt more for this man after our conversation, and I wanted to be close to him. I wanted him inside me, filling me.

I needed distraction, so I chose the thing I hated the most and started doing some laundry. I'd let it pile up too long and a chore was the best alternative for sitting around and replaying all that had happened.

But I wished Max was there.

And ten minutes later my heart did a little flutter when I heard a knock at the door. Had I willed him to turn around and come back? Had I wished into existence the sight of him standing in my doorway, telling me he wanted to stay the night?

I got to the door and couldn't unlock it fast enough. I stopped just before opening it, closed my eyes, took a deep breath, but couldn't stop the ear-to-ear smile on my face.

I opened the door and the fluttering in my heart turned to a pounding—a scary thumping in my ears and throat, my body's instant fight or flight reaction to the sight of Chris standing there.

What felt like hours couldn't have even been minutes. It could only have been mere seconds until he spoke.

"Hear me out."

That's all he said. I stood there stunned, my mouth going dry, my heart still thundering in my chest. I didn't say anything.

"Look, Olivia, I know this might seem strange—"

"You're goddamn right it is." I started to close the door, but he stuck his foot in the way too fast. I quickly reached up and fastened the chain. It wasn't a very good barrier, but it was my only choice at the moment. "I swear to God I'll call the police if you don't leave."

He didn't move. "Just hear me out, okay? I'm sorry."

"Sorry? For what? For stalking me? For freaking out on me? For almost hitting me? For stalking me *all the way out here*? Go away. Forever!"

I pushed on the door, trying to make him move his foot, but he didn't budge.

"I drove all the way here to talk to you. I'm not going away until you talk to me."

"You're going away," the voice said.

Through the narrow opening in the door, I saw Chris look to his left. "Who the hell are *you*?"

Chris was suddenly gone. In a flash I saw Max's body shove him out of the way. I unchained the door and poked my head out. Max and Chris were on the sidewalk. Max was getting the better of him. One punch to the face and Chris seemed dazed.

Max rose from the ground, pulling Chris up with him. Max looked at me. "Chris, right?"

I nodded.

The front of Chris's shirt was bunched in Max's fists. Max shook him and threw him against the wall, then moved to stand in front of him.

I peered around the corner so I could see them again.

Chris said, "You broke my nose."

"You're lucky."

"Who the hell are you?"

Max said, "I'm the guy who's going to make it my mission to destroy your pathetic fucking life if you don't leave Olivia alone."

Chris covered his face with one hand. Blood was running down his wrist. For once, Chris was telling the truth—Max really had broken his nose.

"Do you understand me?"

Chris looked at his bloody hand.

Max raised his fist and drew it back behind his head. "Does this look familiar?"

Chris looked at me. I kept my eyes trained on Max.

"Do you understand?" Max repeated.

Chris said, "Is this your boyfriend or something?"

I didn't say anything.

Max made a move like he was going to release the punch, but he didn't have time.

Chris put his hands up in front of him. "All right. Jesus, man! I'll go!" Chris started to walk away, backwards down the walkway, as if he were afraid to let Max get behind him. There's nothing like the sight of a frightened bully.

Max watched him as he got to the end of the sidewalk, then walked down there himself and saw to it that Chris got in his car and left.

When Max got back to my door he said, "I'm taking you with me."

I threw my arms around his neck and hugged. “How did you know he was here?”

“I got out to the parking lot and saw a guy sitting in a car looking at the building. When I drove past, I saw the Ohio plates. Your ex-boyfriend is a moron, Olivia.”

“I can stay here. I don’t think he’ll come back after—”

“Please don’t argue with me about this. I want you by my side tonight. Pack an overnight bag and come with me.”

TEN

During the drive to his house, it dawned on me to let Krystal know what had happened. If she was going to be alone in the apartment I had to let her know the details. I got her voicemail and hung up. Ten minutes later, when we were almost to Max’s place, I called again and left a message, then texted her so she’d be sure to get the info.

I mentioned to Max what a strange lifestyle Krystal seemed to have—disappearing for days on end, hardly ever home to begin with, and when she is home she more often than not has a different guy with her.

Max just shrugged it off. "The important thing is, you're with me."

I leaned over and rested my head on his shoulder until we got to his house.

Once inside he said, "I have six bedrooms."

"No need to brag."

He laughed. "I wasn't bragging."

"I know."

I appreciated the gesture. He was letting me know I could sleep anywhere I wanted. "I think it's very gentlemanly of you to give me the option. So does that mean I can do what I want?"

"Absolutely."

During one of our talks, he'd mentioned that he had a movie theater in his house. I had laughed at the time, and he said he was serious—it wasn't a full-size theater, but it sat twenty people and that's where he watched dailies and screened movies for friends.

"I want to see this theater you told me about."

He smiled, took my hand, and led me to a door just off the den. We walked down a flight of stairs and, sure enough, there it was: a miniature theater.

"Don't tell me you want to watch a movie," he said.

"No, I had something else in mind."

We were standing between the screen and the first row of seats. My back was to the screen; Max was facing me, with a seat just a foot or so behind him. I put my hand flat on his chest and pushed. The backs of his knees touched the chair, and he sat.

Max's eyes squinted, like he was trying to figure out what had gotten into me. That, or he knew, and he was turned on by me showing how much I wanted him.

I dropped to my knees in front of him.

"Olivia…" His voice faded out.

I shook my head. "Don't try to stop me."

I unfastened his belt, unbuttoned his pants, and unzipped them, all while keeping eye contact with Max. I loved watching the thrill in his eyes.

I slid my hand into his boxers and felt him get harder under my touch. I stroked him, feeling his length and girth growing. He was hard and warm.

"I want you, Olivia."

I shook my head. "Uh-uh. This is payback for that afternoon in your office, Mister."

I lowered his pants and freed his erection. It sprang out and stood before me, long and thick, the visible veins flooded to make it so hard.

Without using my hands, I lowered my head and took the head into my mouth.

Max groaned.

My lips puckered and caressed the plump crown. I held the tip in my mouth and made little circles with my tongue.

I put my hand on his chest and felt the vibration when he moaned deeply.

I released the head, and ran my tongue down his impressive length, feeling every contour of his cock. I ran my tongue along the base of it from below, and then around the top, his erection under my chin and touching my neck. I licked up the top side of it, back to the head, where I took him into my mouth again and eased him in as far as it would go.

"Jesus, Olivia. You're making me crazy."

I moaned as my sucking picked up speed. My head bobbed in his lap and I felt his hand gently cup the side of my head. He ran his fingers around the edge of my ear, sending a shiver down my neck, making my nipples hard.

Max's thumb was on my cheek. His cock was halfway in my mouth, and my head was lolling from side to side, a sort of twisting motion. His thumb moved to the edge of my mouth, then traced the outline of my lips. He was feeling his cock sliding in and out of my mouth.

I looked up and watched his facial expressions—his mouth in the shape of an O, his eyes half-closed under lids heavy with the fog of pleasure, and the way he tilted his head to get a different view.

His hand left my face and rested on the arm of the chair. He reclined a little farther back.

"I'm sure you've had lots of these in here," I said, stroking him just with my hand. I purposely said it as a statement, but meant it as a question.

"Never."

"Never in here, or never…"

His answer came out almost just as a breath: "Never in a movie theater."

I'd been a little worried about not being enough for Max, considering he was a little older and certainly had more experience than me. The thought that I was able to be a first for him at anything was thrilling.

I took him in my mouth again.

"No hands," he said.

The commanding tone in his voice would have been enough to get me wet if I hadn't already been so turned on. But this was all about Max right now.

I put both hands on his thighs. His cock was standing free, my mouth sealed around the head. I could taste the first droplet of pre-cum.

Max started moving his hips, stroking himself across my lips and tongue. I loved that I could make him move that way. His cock grew thicker, swelling in response to the sensation of fucking my mouth.

I concentrated on his pleasure—swirling my tongue across the head of his cock as he thrust into my mouth, tightening my lips around him.

I heard Max's breathing get heavy and deep. I looked up and saw him staring intently at my face.

"Olivia…"

I moved my head with more intensity, his cock slipping across my tongue. I was driven to pull every drop of bliss from him.

Max's hand was again on the side of my head. His fingers combed deep into my hair.

"I'm close to coming."

I wanted it. Badly. Wanted to feel, taste, and swallow, as though it was another way of experiencing his power.

Max stopped thrusting. I felt his cock twitch and begin to pulsate. Then a thick stream of semen, and another.

He groaned: "Ah, God…."

I looked at his face, but his head was thrown back against the headrest.

He kept coming, as though he hadn't in a while and the release would never end.

The way his body reacted to me, the words and noises he spoke, his every response to the way I made him come was the most pleasing thing I could have had that night.

I cleaned him with my tongue, and when I was finished I tucked him back into his pants. He was still semi-hard.

"Don't put it away," he said. "We're not done yet."

"Oh yes we are."

He looked at me quizzically. "I want to make you come, Olivia."

I shook my head with a little smile on my face as I zipped up his pants. "I know you do, but I'm not going to let you. I told you this is payback for that little number you did on me in your office."

"You didn't have to pay me back, as you put it."

"I know I didn't have to. I *wanted* to." I stood. "Now, come on. Let's go upstairs."

I loved the fact that he wanted to get me off. But what I loved more was the knowledge that I could give to him while at the same time taking what I wanted. Besides, I knew the next time we had sex he'd probably blow my mind.

Max rose to his feet and pressed his mouth to mine. It was the first time a guy had kissed me after getting a blowjob. In my experience—which wasn't all that much, admittedly—guys wouldn't go anywhere near a girl's mouth after they came in it. But Max was different. So very different.

I had to break away from the kiss because it carried the great risk of getting me all worked up and then I'd fall prey to his seduction. And I really did want this to be all about him.

"Let's go." I ran across the theater floor, like a little kid again, and made my way up the steps.

Max was right behind me, saying, "You amaze me, you know that?"

Later, as I got into his bed, I began to worry about the incident with Chris.

Max and I were lying on our sides, facing each other.

"What if he sues you?" I asked.

"He won't."

"How do you know? You're worth…what, millions? Why wouldn't he?"

Max ran a finger along my cheek. "Everything would come out. He won't take that risk."

"I guess you're right."

"Relax. Everything's going to be fine."

"If that's true," I said, "then why did you insist that I stay here with you?"

"It was spur of the moment, with everything that happened. But now it's convenient because tomorrow we're going to do something I know you've never done."

"What's that?"

The possibilities were endless with Max Dalton. It would have been a waste of time and energy to even begin to guess what he had in mind.

"I'm taking you somewhere for the weekend," he said. "We'll stop by your place in the morning and pick up whatever you need."

"Where are we going?"

"It's a surprise."

"I hate surprises," I said. "I mean, I hate the suspense."

"Remember the last time I told you I had a surprise?"

Remember? How could I forget? He'd whisked me away and I had the best sex of my life that night.

"Refresh my memory," I said, faking a frown.

Max just smiled. "Very funny."

He fell asleep before I did. I had my back to him and he held me tightly. I listened to his deep, even breathing. I was exhausted, but I wanted to stay awake and crystallize this feeling forever in my mind.

It felt good. It felt right.

At least for a little while....

FADE INTO ME

ONE

I'm not sure how to explain how weird it was the next morning to be cruising through Los Angeles in Max's convertible Porche 911. It was strange because I felt so free and elated, but in the back of my mind there was still the chill of fear from the incident with Chris.

What had started off as a terrifying evening had turned into a night of mind-blowing sex with Max, and there I was the next morning being whisked off to the California wine country.

He didn't tell me where we were going, at first. He just drove to the small Bob Hope Airport outside of Burbank, where many Hollywood stars kept private planes.

I was in awe when he told me the plane belonged to him. I halfway expected him to tell me he had chartered a flight for us or something. I'm not sure why. Max was loaded. He was a Hollywood bigshot. So why shouldn't he have his own airplane?

"But I don't fly it," he said.

"Oh, well then I'm not as impressed."

He caught my sarcasm and smiled. "Just get on the plane. *My* plane."

And that's what I did, gleefully bounding up the steps as Max followed me, patting me on the ass once.

When we got off the ground, we had a great view of the California coast. Being from the Midwest, I had never had much experience with beaches. I'd found the California coast, what little I'd seen of it, to be breathtaking. The aerial view was even more gorgeous.

Max had arranged for breakfast to be on the flight, and about thirty minutes into the trip, we were drinking orange juice and coffee, and sharing a truly sinfully large plate of French toast with berries and cream and syrup.

"Are you trying to make me fat so no one else will want me?"

Max eyed me up and down. "One plate of French toast isn't going to make you fat."

I threw my napkin at him. "Jerk. You know that wasn't the point of the question."

He swallowed the last of his bite of breakfast with a smile on his face, took a sip of OJ and said, "I don't care if someone else wants you. They're not going to take you away from me."

"Welcome to Napa," Max said as we landed.

Having heard of the place throughout my life, but having never been there, it existed only as a fantasy in my mind. Sort of the same way I felt about Max. But he was real. So was Napa. And we were here for what promised to be an amazing weekend.

Max had a car waiting for us at the airport—nothing fancy or flashy, just a good old fun Jeep, which Max drove like he'd just stolen the thing.

We zipped along roads that snaked through the wine vineyards. Max was like a tour guide, telling me all kinds of details about the various wineries we cruised past.

We finally ended up at a cottage on the side of a hill. It was private, nestled in a patch of trees. I got out of the car and looked around, breathing in the crisp, fresh air.

"Come on," Max was saying as I gazed out at the countryside, taking in the view. "There's plenty of time for sight-seeing. What I want now is you, inside."

"Why, Mr. Dalton," I said, affecting a fake patrician accent, "whatever do you have in mind?"

I was trying to be playful. We'd had our fun with banter and teasing during the trip up here. I expected him to continue with the light-heartedness. But he didn't.

"What I have in mind, beautiful Olivia, is you...naked, on the bed, so I can have my way with you."

He stepped toward me and before I knew it, his mouth was on mine. My lips parted, letting his tongue slide in.

Max lifted me up and I wrapped my legs around his waist, locking my ankles behind his back. He walked us over to the couch. Something about this man and couches...

He set me down gently, and I felt his erection pressing between my legs.

"Let's get these off of you." He unbuttoned my slacks, unzipped them, and started working them down my hips and my legs. When he kissed me again, he made a moaning sound deep in his chest, almost a growl, mixed with his warm breath against my lips.

Max ran his hands up the insides of my legs, and slipped a finger under the elastic of my panties. We held eye contact as I arched into his touch and felt his finger make contact with my clit.

"Already getting wet," he said.

"You have that effect on me."

He kissed me again, hard, passionately, taking my tongue into his mouth and sucking on it. His finger stayed right on my clit, working perfect little circles around in the slickness. Then he used his thumb to rub my clit, and I felt him slip a finger inside me, then a second one.

Our foreheads were touching and I looked deep into his eyes as he teased me so completely. Max licked at my lips, then said, "I'm going to get you to the point where you beg me to fuck you."

"I'm already there," I said, without hesitation.

He shook his head slightly. "No, not yet. I'll be the judge."

Max resumed kissing me as his fingers explored inside, finding the spot that made me squirm. He knew he had me. He kept rubbing right there as I writhed beneath him.

Fuck. This guy knew how to make me come so good, so easily. Usually, anyway....

He stopped and raised up, kneeling on the couch. He pulled his shirt over his head. I loved watching the way his muscles moved beneath his skin.

He stood, unbuckled his belt, unzipped his pants, and was quickly standing there totally naked. Each time I saw him I was more in awe of his beautiful body. And this seemed like he was enjoying the way I looked at him, as he just stood there—totally exposed to me, his hard cock raging with lust.

"Sit up," he said.

The commanding tone in his voice sent a tingle through my body. Never before had I been with a man who could have spoken to me like that without igniting a little resentment in me, or even eliciting some laughter. But with Max…well, he was different in countless ways.

He stepped toward me and, wordlessly, guided his cock toward my mouth. I opened and felt the head slip just past my lips.

"Suck me there."

Again, the blunt commanding nature of his words urged me to please him.

The head of his cock was nestled between my pursed lips. I sucked gently, then moved my tongue in a circular motion around it. A droplet of precome was my reward.

"You look so beautiful doing that. Take it all now."

Max put his hand on the side of my head—his palm on my cheek, his fingers pointing downward and curling under my chin. He held my head in place as he moved back forth, slowly, fucking my mouth.

I felt his cock grow harder and bigger as it slid in and out of my mouth.

Max pulled it out after a minute or so. "Look what you do to me, Olivia."

His erection was thick, full, appearing to be on the verge of erupting right there in front of my face. It was slick and glistening from my sucking. Pointing straight out and up a little. Eager. Ready.

Max moved toward me, bent down, and kissed me vigorously. "Lie back."

I repositioned myself the way he wanted.

He lowered himself to his knees in front of me, and in less than two seconds his mouth was on me. His tongue parted me and slipped into my wet hole. Damnit, I could come just from being tongue-fucked by Max. But I didn't want to yet. I wanted it to build up slowly before the release.

"Don't come yet," he said, as if he were able to read my mind. And, well hell, judging by everything else he was able to do to and with me, maybe he could read it.

Max's lips encircled my clit. He sucked it into his mouth and my hips pushed upward to meet his face.

I looked down at him. His eyes were wide open, looking right back up at me. He'd been watching my reaction. Just then, he slipped a finger inside me again, curling it so it hit that spot he had found earlier. I clenched around his finger as he rubbed me.

He pulled his face away, but kept fucking me with his finger. Just the one at first, but then another joined it. My vision was going foggy from the pleasure, but I was able to look down my body and see him still looking at me. Watching me as I writhed on the couch and grabbed one of the throw pillows so tightly I probably could have torn it open.

I didn't think my voice would work, but I found out it did when I involuntarily said, almost shouted, "Fuck me, Max. Fuck me!"

Just like he had said: he would get me to the point of begging him to fuck me.

And finally, mercifully, that's what he did...

With the condom rolled on, he pushed into me slowly. Deep. Then hard, all the way to the hilt. There was a little stab of pain as he stretched me, but it quickly turned to pleasure.

Just like the last time we fucked, Max again gathered both of my wrists in his strong hand and pinned my arms up over my head on the back of the couch. I was rocking back and forth from his thrusts, which were picking up speed and intensity. I could see on his face how much he wanted me, needed me, had to have me lying there with my legs spread open for him to take me however he wanted…and it was the sexiest look I'd ever seen on a man's face.

"Tell me how it feels."

I was almost breathless but I managed: "Perfect."

He rammed into me harder, then stopped, his face just a couple of inches from mine. "*You* are perfect." Max dropped his head and took a nipple into his mouth, sucking it in hungrily, then running his tongue around the edge of it, flicking his tongue across it, drawing it to full hardness. Then he sealed his lips around my other nipple, and applied pressure as he held it between his tongue and upper teeth—soft on one side, rough edge on the other, pleasure and a little pain.

I had been holding my breath and finally had to let it out and take another one. I hadn't even realized I'd been doing it. Damn, how far had I let myself go that I forgot to breathe when he was doing these things to me?

He let go of my wrists, then wrapped his hand around my ankle and lifted it up in front of him, then over, so I was lying on my side.

He was still buried deep in me.

"Say my name."

I didn't have the breath power to say anything—my lungs were working overtime, almost panting.

"Say my name, Olivia."

"Ma-Max..."

"Olivia."

"Max."

His thrusting increased, harder and deeper. "Olivia."

Under any other circumstances, being with someone and repeating each other's names back and forth would have been silly. A child's game. But this was well outside the realm of play. It was a verbal connection. Just the two of us, alone, fucking, calling out to each other.

Max was kneeling on the floor and with me lying on my side on the couch, he was lined up perfectly. He had one hand on my thigh, one on my ass, as he drove into me.

I clutched the pillow and brought it to my face. I wanted to scream from the unreal sensation and I wanted the sound muffled. But Max reached up and pulled the pillow away.

"I want to hear you."

As I moaned and breathed heavily, Max leaned down over me. He turned me on my stomach and lowered me to my knees on the floor, my arms still on the couch.

From behind, he slid deeper into me as his hips bumped against my ass.

"Let it out, Olivia."

I screamed and "Oh!" and then "Yes!" and then his name.

"That's it."

Max brushed my hair to one side, exposing my neck. I felt his lips on my neck, sucking on my skin, then the hard edge of his teeth grazed along me.

Fuck. It was like he was trying to devour me, consume all of me...

His mouth still on my neck, he reached around my hip. I felt one of his fingers zero in right on my clit, and he began making circles around it. I dropped my head to the couch and just let go—all control fully ceded to Max.

"Come for me," he whispered. "Now."

I couldn't hold back. In a flash, the orgasm's prelude flushed through my body, and my pussy was in spasms around his cock.

He slowed his thrusts, riding my orgasm slowly. And then I felt his cock throb and pulsate. Then his breath exhaling harder on my neck—hot and steamy.

"Fuck..." he groaned as he began to come.

TWO

I would have been content to take a little nap after that round of incredible sex, but Max was eager to show me around the vineyards. He also said he was famished, which I began to suspect was the real reason he was in a hurry to go out somewhere. What is it with men who have to eat after sex? Something animalistic, perhaps. Judging by Max's ferocity on the couch earlier, I guess that's a good assumption.

We showered together. Max washed my hair—an extremely intimate and erotic thing, in my book. I loved the way my hands slipped and slid all over his naked, lathered-up body. Forget the nap idea; I could have stayed in that shower all day.

But there was so much to do, so much to see.

We had lunch at a California cuisine restaurant, out on the deck, overlooking fields of grapes that seemed to go on forever.

"How is it?"

We had moved on from the salad to sharing a flatbread with fresh local tomatoes, artichoke hearts, onions, mushrooms, topped off with herbs and a layer of fresh house-made mozzarella.

"Amazing," I said. "I almost wouldn't even call it pizza."

"Healthiest kind there is. More wine?"

I nodded but didn't speak, having taken another bite already.

We enjoyed a few moments of silence and then I asked Max if he still wrote movies.

He looked at me and frowned. "All the time."

"Are you going to make any of them?"

Max sipped his wine, set it on the table, and a heavy sigh left his mouth. "Probably not."

"Why?"

"I just write for myself now. I think I've said all I wanted to say in my movies that got made."

There was something on his face that told me he didn't want to talk about it. Maybe a kind of regret, or remorse, or…maybe exhaustion.

"I'm not sure how much longer I'm going to do this," he said. And quickly, he added, "But that's between you and me."

I wondered if the movie he was making with our client, Jacqueline Marthers, would be his last. I had read the script and thought it would make an amazing movie. To think that I had played some small part in the creation of what may be

Max Dalton's last movie was thrilling and chilling at the same time.

More importantly, though, was the fact that he had apparently shared a secret with me. He trusted me enough to tell me he was thinking about getting out of the business. There was no way I'd breach his confidence.

"Okay," I said, "so you write for yourself. Do you have all these scripts lying around somewhere?"

"Not lying around." He smiled. "I keep them all in a desk drawer. Which," he added, "is locked, so don't think about stealing them and selling them on eBay."

"What?!"

Max laughed heartily. "God, you're fun to tease, you know that?"

"We have good banter."

"Yes, we do."

He lifted his wine, we clinked glasses, and drank.

We spent at least another lazy hour there, looking out over the vineyard, looking at each other, making mostly small talk. That is, until he brought up Chris.

"What's he capable of?"

I shrugged. "What do you mean?"

"You told me what he did that night, but is there more?"

"No."

His eyebrows rose. "Honest?"

"Honest. And I'd rather not talk about him right now."

"Olivia, if I'm going to protect you, I need to know—"

"I don't need you to protect me," I said, a bit more acidly than I had intended. "If he comes back, I'll call the cops."

Max shook his head. "They won't do anything. At least not until he crosses a major line and tries to hurt you, or actually hurts you."

I knew he was right. Plus, there was the whole aspect of keeping this from my family.

By this time, however, now that Chris had showed up in LA, I began to think there probably was more depth to his obsessively controlling anger. But what was I going to do? Express that fear to Max? Then what? I didn't exactly know what Max was capable of, either. I really just wanted Chris to go away, back to Ohio, and stay there.

Equally as much, I wanted the *topic* of Chris to go away. This was supposed to be a fantasy getaway weekend. It had started that way, but Max's worries about Chris had derailed it. I needed to get things back on track.

"Tell me more about you."

He looked at me. "What do you want to know?"

I thought about it for a second, then said, "Everything."

"That's a lot."

"Are we in a hurry?"

Max smiled and sipped from his wine. Then he told me his life story.

THREE

It turns out he, too, was from the Midwest. So we had that in common. That day I met him and later went to research him on the Internet, I hadn't seen any birth info, other than his age. His Wikipedia page had been mostly professional data, which interested me then, but now I needed to know more about Max the man, not Max the Hollywood big-shot.

He was an only child; his father was a men's clothing salesman, his mother a teacher, both of whom wanted Max to go to college and obtain a business degree. But Max had no interest in that.

Most of his teen years were spent in movie theaters and libraries, absorbing film and literature. He was totally enthralled with the idea of a cast of characters and a story coming out of seemingly nowhere. He said he could remember nights in bed, staring at the ceiling, in complete wonderment that great movies and great books began with a blank page, and someone's thoughts and wishes and desires filled the pages in the form of the characters and a story.

Something from nothing. Even the bad movies and bad books were the products of someone's hard work and imagination, so in Max's mind they deserved his respect, even if they didn't personally appeal to him.

He began filling notebooks with ideas—plots, characters, scenes—all a big jumble of things that flowed from his mind when pen hit paper. It's how he spent the vast majority of his free time. Even some of the time that he was supposed to be studying.

When he turned sixteen, he stopped going to church, to the great disappointment of his parents. It wasn't that he was rejecting his upbringing so much as he had a new focus. All he wanted to do was write, and any time he spent not doing that was, in his mind, wasted time. When he announced his desire to stop spending two or three hours every Sunday at the church, a huge argument erupted, and he left home for three days.

"I had to go back. I had no money, and home was where the food was," he told me with a grin.

His parents were happy to have him home, at least for the first night. The next day they began to issue instructions: more schoolwork, less time playing around with what his father called "time-wasting writing," and the obligatory demand to keep going to church.

Max gave in. He kept going to church, but spent most of the time writing in his head. That's when he realized he had a memory like a steel trap—he could write in thoughts, even edit in thoughts, and when he got home he would frantically scribble them down in a whirl of excitement.

"It was a rush," he said. "The fact that I could do that was just more proof to me that I was born to be a writer."

So it all worked out for the time being. Then came the inevitable battle with his parents over where he would go to college. They, of course, wanted him to go to a local state school, where his father would have gone if he'd had the intelligence and the money back when he was Max's age. Max was unyielding in his desire to go to film school. His parents said there was no way they were going to pay for him to go all the way to UCLA, where Max wanted to start his undergrad work and then apply to the film school for his junior year, as the admission requirements stated.

His parents hadn't even wanted him to apply to UCLA, but he'd sent off the application along with the fee, paid for out of his savings from his part-time job at the movie theater.

It was during this argument that his parents confessed to taking his UCLA application out of the mailbox all those months ago. Max couldn't believe it.

Alone with his dad one afternoon while his mother was at the grocery store, Max confronted him. "Stop hitting mom."

Max's father turned to face him. "What are you going to do about it?"

Max stepped closer to his father, and looked down at him. By this time in his life, Max was about an inch taller than his father. He also outweighed him by at least twenty pounds—all of it muscle.

"Touch mom again and you'll find out what I'm going to do about it."

Max's father laughed, but said nothing.

"And there's always the police," Max added.

"So," his father said, "what are you going to do? Blackmail me?"

Max just laughed and left the room. His father had been such an asshole to him, never giving Max the freedom he wanted or needed, always treating him like he was incapable of doing anything right, taking his belt to Max, or swatting him with the back of his hand, which stung due to Max's father's fake college class ring (an item he wore to impress people). Well, now that had all changed. Max had the upper hand on his father.

Max knew what he had to do, and he hatched his plan over the next couple of weeks.

He would leave home, taking the three hundred and sixty-one dollars he had to his name, and hitchhike halfway across to the country to Hollywood. But that probably wouldn't be enough.

He'd never thought of blackmailing his father before he himself raised the possibility. Now it was looking like a damn good idea. Especially since Max had something else on his father. So, two days before Max skipped town, he went to the store where his father worked and said he needed five-thousand dollars.

His father didn't ask any questions. He simply wrote the check. After all, what was he going to say when Max told him he knew about Annette and Roberta, the two women his father had had affairs with (Roberta was still in the picture, as far as Max had been able to determine). Max's dad didn't even look shocked, didn't ask how Max knew.

When Max was leaving the office, he turned around and looked at his father. His dad's eyes were weary, and he appeared to have given up all hope of having a normal relationship with his son.

Two days before his seventeenth birthday, Max told his mother to pack her favorite stuff, but only two bags. On the morning of his birthday, after his father left for work, Max and his mother boarded a Greyhound bus. It was bound for southern California. It was on this bus ride that Max's mother said she always wanted him to do what he wanted, and only agreed with his father because of the hold he had on her. Max said he knew all along.

Over the next three years, Max worked in movie theaters, restaurants, and gas stations, while he finished high school. His mother got a job as a teacher's assistant at a middle school.

He finally landed a job that interested him: as a PA announcer on a tourist bus. He had impressed the owner of the tour bus company with his vast, almost obsessive knowledge of Hollywood. This led to him making a connection with someone who worked as a junior production assistant at MGM studios. His foot was in the door.

Max started leaving his original scripts lying around the studio—in various conference rooms, mail-slots, under windshields of cars parked in spots that were marked with the names of bigwigs.

That's how he sold his first script. He was a true self-made screenwriter, without an agent, and all before he had turned twenty years old.

By the time he was twenty-five he had three blockbuster films, an Oscar nomination, and the next step was moving into directing and producing. But he hadn't been happy since.

"And," he told me, "to this day I've never told my mom that I knew about my dad's cheating."

"You could have ruined him."

He nodded his head. "I know. But it would have ruined my mom, too. But she's happy now. She lives in Thousand Oaks. Not too far from me, but not too close, either. She didn't want to be right in the heart of all the Hollywood action."

"And your dad?"

"Haven't heard anything about him in years."

We were getting tired of sitting at the table, so Max suggested we take a walk through the vineyard. It occurred to me that throughout the whole story he had just told me, he didn't mention any girlfriends.

FOUR

Rather than go out to eat, Max grilled salmon and made a giant salad, and we ate on the floor of the lodge. The original plan was to have an evening picnic, but the weather brought an unexpected—and rare—rain shower.

Max's culinary skills turned out to be as impressive as everything else he did. The food was delicious, and the setting was romantic. Just the two of us sitting on a large blanket, a roaring fire going, and Harry Connick Jr. tunes providing the soundtrack.

Later, Max wowed me again. But this time we were in his bed. I had three orgasms to his one, and I teased him later that it seemed like a fair ratio.

Sunday morning, I woke to an empty bed. I called out for Max, thinking he might be in another room, but got no response. I got out of the bed, wrapped the sheet around me, walked through the den, and looked out on the large deck. No Max to be seen.

I looked around for a note. Nothing.

I was beginning to worry when I heard the door open and he came in, sweaty and catching his breath. "Morning."

"Hey. Where were you?"

"Went for a run. I was about a mile away when I realized I should have left a note in case you woke up. Sorry."

I moved toward him.

"I'm all sweaty."

"I don't care," I said, wrapping my arms around him. The sheet dropped to the floor, leaving me standing there naked.

Max kissed me on the cheek, pushed me away gently, looked me up and down and said, "You're wearing my favorite thing."

Before I could respond, I heard my cell phone ringing. I got it out of my purse. It was Krystal calling. If she hadn't been my roommate, I might have just let it go to voicemail. But I answered it.

"Are you okay?" she blurted.

"I'm fine. Why?"

"You haven't been here all weekend. I was getting worried."

I didn't have the speakerphone on, but the volume was loud enough and the room was quiet enough so that Max could hear Krystal. I looked at him and rolled my eyes. Krystal, worried about me? I was surprised she even noticed I was gone.

"Nothing to worry about. I'm in Napa."

"Ohhh, nice. With Max?"

"Yes."

"Well, I'll let you get back to doing him—I mean, I'll let you get back to him." She laughed.

"Okay," I said, "I'll be home later sometime today."

We stayed in Napa for lunch and went on a private tour of one of the oldest wineries in the area, escorted by the founder's grandson who looked to be about Max's age or early thirties at the most. His wife joined us, and more than once I caught her looking at Max in a way that was pretty risky considering her husband was standing right there.

It might have bothered me at some point in my life. Maybe even just a few weeks ago. But I was getting more comfortable in the feeling that Max wanted me and only me, so I didn't care how she looked at him. Plus, the way Max was holding on to me made me think he noticed it, too, and might have been reassuring me.

It sounds ridiculous, I know. After all, what could he have possibly done? Lost me somewhere on the grounds of the winery, found a way to distract her husband, and gone off somewhere private and fuck her?

But Max knew how uneasy I was. I had expressed to him in no uncertain terms that I doubted my ability to keep up with his style of life. So far, though, I'd been doing just fine. But I still like to think his tight hold on me was a signal…not so much for her, but for me.

On the plane ride home, I raised the subject I had avoided the day before and asked him about his love life.

"I thought we were going to nap on the way home," he said.

"When did we decide that?"

"We didn't. I did."

"Okay," I said. "Well, I veto the idea. So start talking."

He was good natured about me being so forward. Which is exactly what I expected. Otherwise I wouldn't have gone there.

Max's first girlfriend was a girl named Denise. They were fifteen when they started dating, and sixteen when they had sex. It was the first time for both of them. Max admitted to being a fumbling ball of nerves during the act, and to freaking out when he saw a spot of blood on the sheet when Denise got up to go to the restroom afterward.

"Cherry-popper," I said, hitting him lightly on the shoulder.

"You say that like I'm guilty of something." He looked at me, an uncharacteristically sheepish look on his face.

"Well, aren't you?"

"No more than the guy who popped yours," he retorted. "Why don't you tell me about him?"

"No, no. *You* go on."

He laughed. "That's what I thought."

I didn't want to talk about the time I lost my virginity. It was unremarkable. Actually, quite a boring story. I was older than Denise had been when she lost hers, and the guy was no Max Dalton. God, how I wished it had been Max that night....

I let go of the fleeting thought and focused on the rest of his story....

Denise cheated on him with a wide receiver on the football team. He never spoke to her again. Shortly after that, he met Katherine, and within two months they were talking marriage and kids. This was during his junior year in high school, and Katherine was much like my sister—wanting to get married young, have kids, settle down. Max played along for a while, figuring there was no harm and that he wasn't leading her on. After all they were teenagers.

Their relationship ended when he left town, of course.

Once in California, he dated, but nothing serious. Mostly surfer girl groupies, the bleach-blonde bunnies who kick up sand all day while fit, tanned, athletic boys show off their board skills. Max wasn't that great at surfing but, he said, the girls liked him anyway.

"Yeah, I bet," I said. "Who could resist you?" I squeezed his bicep.

"Turns out a lot of girls could."

"Oh, go on…"

"There's nothing really interesting," he said. "I haven't been serious with anyone in quite a while."

"Do you want to get married?"

He looked at me. "Are you proposing?"

I blurted out an indelicate laugh. "You know what I mean."

"Yeah. Marriage? I don't know. I guess it's just a matter of being with the right person."

"Well, sure."

"No," he said. "I mean the desire. How can someone just want to get married? I think you really only have that desire when you're with the right person. Nobody knows if they want to be married, as some kind of abstract idea. You don't know what it's like, and if you're not with someone you'd marry, how can the thought even be serious?"

There was a pause and I guessed he was waiting for me to answer. "I think you're over-thinking it."

"Hmm. Maybe. All that matters is that you're here."

We were quiet the rest of the way back to Los Angeles. We hit some turbulence about ten minutes out, but otherwise it was a smooth flight.

Smooth in the physical sense, at least. Emotionally, things were a little rocky.

I didn't want the weekend with Max to end. Tomorrow would mean back to the grind. And while I loved the work I was doing, it would be an extreme understatement to say I was distracted by thoughts of being with Max all the time.

On the opposite end of the emotional spectrum, I was a little nervous about Max being so vague and dismissive about his relationships with women during recent years. I knew it was probably nothing more than him sparing me lurid tales of encounters with Hollywood's hottest, horniest, and most desperate female starlets and socialites.

If that's what he was doing, then he did the right thing. I really didn't want to know about those women. All I wanted to do was see where this was going with Max. And, so far, he'd given me no real reason to be afraid. He had done and said absolutely nothing to make me feel like I wasn't enough for him.

I mentally kicked myself for letting my negativity and self-doubt cap off such a wonderful weekend.

FIVE

Krystal wasn't there when I got home. She hadn't mentioned it on the phone earlier, but I guessed she had to work.

It was a little after 5pm so I decided I should do my regular Sunday check-in with my parents. Mom answered on the first ring. Dad got on the other extension. They asked how my week went, and I filled them in, minus the little jaunt up the coast with Max Dalton, of course.

They were having their kitchen remodeled, so I had to listen to about ten minutes of Mom describing precisely what the contractor was going to do, with Dad piping in every thirty seconds or so complaining about the cost of the new counters, cabinets, and pretty much everything else. A little bickering ensued and Mom finally said they should have that discussion when they're not on the phone with me. Thank God.

"Is Grace around?"

"She's just put the baby down. Let me get her," Mom said.

I really needed to talk to my sister. I'd been putting it off all weekend. I knew if I had called her Friday night, I would have been so angry I probably would have said something I regretted. But now, enough time had passed where I could probably have a rational conversation with her.

When Mom and Dad dropped off the line and it was just Grace, I said, "Did you tell Chris where I was?"

"What? No! I told you I just said LA."

"Then he stalked me."

"He *what*?"

I said, "Chris showed up at my apartment door Friday night."

"Holy shit." The surprise in her voice was genuinely fearful and then changed to regret. "I'm so sorry."

"Yeah."

"It's my fault. Oh my God. I'm so sorry."

Over the next full two minutes or so, she must have apologized a dozen times as I explained what happened. I knew she was truly sorry, but I told her to stop apologizing. I got to the part about how someone saved me, but I didn't tell her who it was, specifically. I just said it was a neighbor.

"I just need you to do something for me," I said, trying to bring this conversation to a close for now.

"Anything. I'll do anything."

Monday morning. I got to my desk without seeing Kevin, thank God. The last thing I needed was my boss asking about my weekend and detecting from my blushing or body-language that I'd been up to something. Of course, he would have no idea I had been with Max. But the ramifications of my dating and sleeping with someone we were working with could have been disastrous for me and my future.

I did finally see Kevin around 11 a.m. He stopped by my desk and said I should pack up my things.

My heart sank. Did he know? Had he found out I had breached his trust by being with Max? I felt my throat go dry and the beginnings of that little stinging you get before you cry, as the tears well up.

"You look like you're going to pass out," he said. "Don't worry. I was joking. Or trying to, anyway. But you do need to pack up your things and come with me."

I stood. "What's going on?"

"Just do it."

He put a box on my desk and started putting things in it. I joined him, and it wasn't long before we were done. There wasn't all that much on my desk. I did make sure to pack up the drawer I used to stash my many packages of sunflower seeds—a snacking habit that caused Kevin to refer to me once as a bird.

He led me down the hall to an office that had been serving as a storage room. He opened the door. All of the extraneous stuff he had been storing in there was gone, and now in its place was a desk, a big leather chair behind it, and two nice visitors' chairs on the other side of the desk.

"I think you earned your own office space," he said, standing aside so I could walk in.

An office of my own. With a window! And out of that window was a view of a good part of Los Angeles. There was a lump in my throat as the realization hit me that I was already moving up in the show business world. Just a few months ago, I could never have dreamed of doing the things I'd already done, and now, with my new office, I felt like I was on my way.

"Wow. Thanks, Kevin." I put my little box of belongings on my new desk.

"You deserve it. Now get settled in and back to work." He smiled and turned down the hallway.

An hour later I was doing yet another interview of an aspiring actress who was seeking representation. Her real name was Madeline Ostrosvky but, like so many others with names that were hard to pronounce, she planned to use a different last name professionally.

"Redford," she said.

"Redford," I repeated flatly.

"It sounds elegant. Like a rich, successful sounding name."

I handled it as gently as I could. "People will think you're trying to capitalize on Robert Redford's name."

"Who?"

Oh, Jesus. Did she really not know who Robert Redford was? I mean, sure, he was of a different generation and it was entirely possible that she hadn't seen any of his movies, even the more recent ones. But what kind of aspiring actor or actress hasn't even heard the name "Robert Redford"?

So I told her who he was, how big a name that is in Hollywood, and repeated my previous warning about it—people would see it as a cheap ploy using Robert Redford's name to make her more recognizable.

"We'll have to work on the name," I concluded, and started to look through more of her resume and photos.

"*We*? Does that mean you're taking me on as a client?"

I paused. This wasn't how we did things at Kevin's agency.

She must not have liked the pause and seen it as bad news, and said, "I really need this. I got these just for acting." She started to lift her blouse. "They're still a little sore—"

"No, no," I said quickly. "You don't have to do that. Really."

That's the kind of afternoon I had. Oh well. At least I had it in my new fancy office.

"I have to go out of town for a few days."

The words from Max coming through the phone disappointed me. It was just before five o'clock and I was sitting at my desk, surveying my new surroundings and wondering what I could do with the walls.

I had become accustomed to seeing Max so often, or at least talking to him every day, I knew I would miss him and it would just make the workdays drag on even more until I laid eyes on him again.

"When?"

"I'm leaving in a couple of hours. Got a couple of people scouting locations for a shoot and they can't seem to agree so I'm going to do it myself."

"Oh, such a take-charge man."

"Do I sense a little sarcasm in your voice?"

I laughed. "No, you sense a *lot*." I loved our banter, and decided to be playful to relieve my disappointment.

"And you," he said, "better watch your mouth or I just might spank you."

My eyebrows rose up my forehead. Thank goodness he couldn't see them. "It's about time you brought that up."

"You like that, huh?"

"My favorite," I said in a hushed voice, trying to sound sexy. The truth was, I had never been spanked. Never even really thought of it. But there was something about the idea of Max doing it that made my insides stir a little. Okay, a lot.

"I'll keep that in mind. You should come with me."

"What?"

"On my trip to New York."

I'd never been to New York City before. I wanted to go so badly. But I knew I couldn't. "I have to work."

"Get out of it."

"I can't, Max. Especially since I have my own office now."

He whistled sarcastically. "Now who's the big-shot in this town?"

"Still you," I said. I told him about the office and how Kevin had presented me with it. "So there's no way I can just take off the rest of this whole week. That would look pretty bad."

"Fine then. We'll go this weekend. I'll come get you and we'll go. I enjoyed our weekend out of town. Nice, quiet—"

"Not so quiet in the bedroom."

"I was getting to that." He chuckled. "So we had the quiet getaway. Now we'll have a not-so-quiet one."

Max and I texted and talked on the phone over the next couple of days. He told me all about his trip and I filled him in on how my week was going. But mostly we talked and teased about our upcoming weekend in New York.

Grace called Wednesday morning as I was driving into work. She had done exactly what I asked her to do.

"He's been to work the last two days," she said.

Several days ago when I told her I had something for her to do, that's what I was talking about. All I wanted was for her to find out if Chris was back home, making me feel safe knowing he was no longer in LA, and that's exactly how I felt upon hearing her news.

"Thank God," I said.

"I think you mean, 'Thank Grace.'"

"Uh, I wouldn't push it if I were you," I said. "You're a big part of the reason all of this happened in the first place."

Her tone shifted to apologetic again, but I told her to forget it.

"Thanks for checking it out," I said. "You still haven't told Mom and Dad, right?"

"No way."

"Good."

"So," she said, changing the subject, "have you met anyone?"

I wanted to tell her about Max. I really did. I just wasn't ready to divulge it to the world yet. And I didn't want her to fret, like I knew she would. She had been just as skeptical of my new life in LA as my parents had been. While my parents were mostly disapproving, Grace was worried about me. All the more reason not to tell her just yet.

SIX

The rest of the week was uneventful. I was glad I didn't have any more interviews with prospective clients. I could focus on my work, which mostly involved coordinating with our PR team to make sure our clients' social media accounts were current. That also involved responding to fans. Before I got this job, I had no idea how much of the interaction between fans and stars was really between fans and PR folks.

When I got home Friday afternoon, there was nothing to do but wait. I had already packed and Max was sending a car for me. He was coming back from Vancouver—all the way to LA to pick me up, then we were off for New York City.

I sat on the couch, using my phone to browse Twitter, all the while thinking about how I had my first flight when I was twenty, and now I was about to take my second private plane ride in as many weekends. What a whirlwind this was turning out to be.

I got a text from Max: Car should be there any minute.

I wrote back: *Great! Can't wait to see you.*

Max: *I'll tell the driver to step on it.*

Me: *Haha. Where are you now?*

Max: *About to land in Burbank. Are you hungry?*

Me: *For you.*

Damn, I shouldn't have sent that. Ah, what the hell—it wasn't like I was playing hard to get anymore.

Max: *You're a bad girl. I like it.*

Me: *I'm not hungry.*

Max: *Too late. I already ordered your food. See you in a bit.*

A few minutes later I was in the backseat of a black Rolls Royce. The driver was an older gentleman named Samuel. He asked me if I'd like a drink on the way. I declined and he closed the door, then whisked us off toward the Burbank airport.

"Excuse me," I said.

"Yes ma'am?"

"Is this…are you…do you work for Max?"

"No, Ms. Rowland. Not directly. I work for myself, actually. Mr. Dalton is one of my clients."

"Oh, okay."

"Sorry to disappoint, ma'am."

I looked at the review mirror and saw him looking back at me. "I'm not disappointed. Sorry if I sounded that way."

"It's quite all right, Ms. Rowland."

"Call me Olivia."

He nodded his head. "I'd rather not, if you don't mind. I like my business to be of the highest class, so while you're free to call me Samuel, or whatever you'd like, I'd prefer to call you Ms. Rowland or ma'am, if you don't mind."

"What's your last name?"

"Garvey."

"Okay, Mr. Garvey, you may call me Ms. Rowland."

"Thank you, ma'am."

"You're welcome, sir."

He didn't laugh out loud, but in the mirror I could see the corners of his eyes scrunch up, so I had at least brought a smile to his face.

By the time we got to the airport it was dusk. A beautiful sunset was at the end of the runway. Max's private plane sat on the tarmac, the door open and the steps down. When Mr. Garvey turned toward the plane, I saw Max standing at the foot of the stairs.

He wore a tight white t-shirt, jeans, and black hiking boots. So simple, yet so fucking hot.

Max came around and opened my door, taking my hand. When I stood next to him, he put his arms around me and gave me the kind of kiss you get when someone hasn't seen you in a long time.

"Wow," I said, when he freed my mouth from his. "You were only gone for a few days."

"I missed you. Come on."

He led me to the plane, up the stairs, and when we boarded I saw that he had several take-out containers from a Chinese place on the table. I really meant what I said earlier—that I wasn't hungry—but all of the sudden I was famished. It smelled so good.

As the plane took off, Max and I looked out the window. I decided that the best way to watch the sunset over the Pacific horizon was from an ascending plane.

"Let's eat," he said.

We ate and talked about New York City. Max knew I had never been there, so he told me all the things he planned to show me over the weekend.

"We barely have two days, though," I said.

"We'll make it count."

The flight would take a little over five hours so after we ate, we settled in together on what turned out to be an extremely comfortable love-seat. With my head on his chest, I fell asleep, and when I woke up I saw that three hours had passed. Max was asleep, and I tried not to wake him as I got up to use the restroom.

When I came out, he was awake.

"I thought you changed your mind about the trip and jumped out," he joked, rubbing his eyes and stretching.

"Well, I couldn't find the parachutes so I went into the bathroom and tried to flush myself down the toilet."

He looked at me straight-faced, then broke out in a hearty laugh.

I sat down close to him, put my head on his shoulder, and my hand on his thigh. I looked down and saw that his jeans were bulging. He had woken up hard.

I moved my hand closer to it and let my fingers graze along the edge of his erection.

Max raised his hand to my chin, turned my face toward his, and kissed me. When his tongue slipped into my mouth, I moved my hand again, this time putting the palm of my hand over the length of the bulge.

"I'm so glad you're here," he said.

"I bet you are. What would you do with this if I wasn't?" I pressed on his cock.

"Same thing I always do when I'm horny and lonely."

"You? Lonely? Doubtful."

He tilted his head. "You make me sound like I'm easy."

I laughed. "No, just not lonely."

He kissed me again.

I felt a strange and unfamiliar rush of boldness and asked, "So how often do you…"

I wasn't making eye contact with him. I was looking at my hand lightly rubbing up and down the length of his erection straining against his jeans.

"Masturbate?" he said, finishing my question for me.

"Sorry. I shouldn't—"

"It's okay. I'll tell you anything you want to know. The answer is: not very often, at least now that I'm spending time with someone I can't get enough of."

"So…" I didn't finish the sentence.

"Yes?"

"Nothing."

Max put his finger under my chin again, turned my face toward his, and said, "You were going to say something or ask something, but you're censoring yourself. You don't have to be shy with me, you know that."

I looked into his eyes. He was so serious, so open to me, almost begging me to finish what I was saying.

"I…I don't know," I said. "I just wondered…I mean, is it good when you do it yourself?"

I felt kind of stupid after I said it. It made me sound so naïve, so inexperienced, so unworldly or something.

"It can be," he said. "It's not as much fun when you're alone."

"Well, it's not like you do that when you're with someone." I laughed at the idea.

Max didn't.

I continued, "Right? I mean, what's the point?"

As he looked at me a little smirk grew out of the corner of his mouth. "You should get rid of your boundaries."

"What are you talking about?"

"Your sexual boundaries."

My mouth fell open. "Uh, excuse me, but I think you should know by now that I don't have any boundaries."

"None?"

I thought about it for a moment. "Well, almost."

He laughed. "See? Boundaries. You have them. That's a shame. You're missing out."

Without speaking, he straightened up in his seat, stood and took my hand. We went to the other side of the plane where two rows of seats faced each other. He stopped at one of the seats. I looked at him. He motioned toward it, still not speaking, but clearly urging me to sit down. I sat.

Max took a step back and lowered into the seat directly across from me. His face was a blank stare—no smiling, no grinning, nothing. But, as with other times when he was turned on, his eyes seemed to have endless depth as he stared back at me.

He leaned back in the seat and lifted his white t-shirt from the hem, showing off his flat, taut stomach. Then, with just the one hand, he started to unbuckle his belt.

I took a deep breath after realizing I'd been holding the air in my lungs.

Max got his belt unfastened, unbuttoned his jeans, and opened the front of his pants. He slipped his fingers under the waistband of his boxers and in one fluid motion, he pushed the front down. His cock sprang free—as hard as I had ever seen it—and his balls appeared full, heavy, loaded for action.

Was I dreaming? I had to make sure I wasn't. The thought of seeing him masturbate for me was making my mouth dry with nervous anticipation while I felt a tingle between my thighs.

Max's hands were on the arms of the seat. His erection stood straight up.

My gaze drifted from his cock to his eyes.

"Hands free?" I joked.

For the first time in several minutes, Max smiled. He didn't say anything, though. He just kept looking at me as my eyes fell once again to take in the view of his magnificent maleness.

When he put his hand on his erection, he used a light touch, stroking it up and down using just his fingertips.

It dawned on me for the first time in my life that since I had never seen a man masturbate, perhaps I didn't fully know what they really liked and wanted. Not that it had ever stopped me from getting results in the past….

Max's hand dipped down and he cupped his balls, rolling them in his hand. I watched with fascination as I realized he wasn't as gentle as I was with them.

He then sat forward a little and took off his shirt, revealing what I had seen several times but still made my eyes glaze over, but not enough to miss out.

Max kicked off his shoes and socks, then wriggled out of his jeans and boxers. And there before me was the most gorgeous view I'd ever had—a naked Max. Now he was the one making himself vulnerable to me.

"What are you thinking?" he asked.

I was at a loss for words for a moment, and he let me gather my thoughts. "I've never seen anything like this."

"Watching a man jerk off?" His right hand grasped his cock and he slowly stroked near the head.

"Never."

"Do you want to?"

Inside my head, I screamed: *Hell yes!* But luckily my filter was in perfect working condition and I gave him the more subdued: "I'd love to."

Max wasn't at all shy about his body. And why should he be? He was in shape, had a nice tan that wasn't overdone as so many are in southern California, and he was well-groomed. Short, neat hair around his cock, not a wild and unruly bush. I knew that from our previous encounters but this was a purely visual experience so it made more of an impact.

I watched the muscles in his arm flex as he stroked up and down. I watched how he tightened his grip near the base, then relaxed it a little as his hand reached the head. There, he made a motion like the was twisting off a bottle-cap.

A droplet formed at the tip of his cock. Max used his thumb to spread it around the head, and more down his shaft. Instant lube.

I wanted to jump him right then and there, but this was something new that he wanted, obviously, so I stayed in my seat. I was starting to squirm a little, though, as I got worked up myself from what I was watching.

Max started stroking himself with two hands, one above the other, still doing that little twist move near the top. I loved it when his hands went down his shaft and the head of his cock poked out from his fist at the top.

"You should join me, Olivia."

In a heartbeat, I thought. I started to move out of my seat but he stopped me.

"No," he said, "let me watch you. We'll watch each other."

Holy shit. I had never masturbated in front of anyone before. I suddenly felt self-conscious, thinking that instead of being hot to watch, I'd probably look stupid.

"Take off your shirt," Max said, and that commanding sultry tone of his was all the encouragement I needed.

I unbuttoned my shirt and for the first time since this started, I thought of the pilot. What if he came back here? He hadn't left the cockpit on our flight to Napa, but this was a long flight. If he had to use the restroom, well, surely there wasn't one up there. He'd have to come back here.

"Don't worry," Max said, once again practically reading my mind.

I didn't take my shirt off, but I did slip my bra off underneath it, much to Max's amusement. Then I finished unbuttoning my shirt.

"Beautiful."

I loved when Max said things like that to me. I pushed my shirt open wider, exposing my breasts to him. I looked down and saw that my nipples were already tightened into hard peaks.

"Touch them," he said.

I cupped them as I watched him stroking himself with a perfect rhythm. I played with my nipples, pinching them, tugging on them, teasing them....

Just as Max was teasing me with that big, beautiful cock. I wanted to drop to my knees and take him into my mouth. Please him. Drive him wild. But he was clearly getting off on this exhibition of mutual masturbation.

"Get naked for me, Olivia."

My heart went to my throat. This was exhilaration beyond anything I could have imagined.

"I need to see your perfect legs. Your perfect pussy. Show me."

I showed him, quickly getting out of my pants and settling back into the seat.

"Put your legs up on the armrests," Max said.

He was now stroking it with just one hand, gripping the head firmly, then sliding down his length, all the way to the base. When his hand reached that point, Max extended his fingers and caressed his balls.

I moved a hand down between my legs to my now-wet folds.

"That's it. So sexy," Max said in a low, gravelly voice.

I watched as the muscles in his chest and arms flexed as he stroked himself. He had become even more wet himself—at one point he gripped his cock just below the head and large bead of precum emerged, running over the back of his fingers. He spread it around the head and all over his shaft.

His upper body wasn't the only part of him flexing. His muscular thighs were tight, the lines of the muscles clearly visible. Same with his calves.

I worked my hand faster, using the tip of my forefinger to make circular motions around my engorged clit.

Damn. I wanted to straddle him and ride him until we both exploded. But I knew I'd get my chance to do that, hopefully many times. And this mutual exhibitionist/voyeuristic getting off was definitely breaking down a boundary that he clearly knew I had.

"Come with me, Olivia."

It didn't take much more encouragement than that. I felt the orgasm building in me, quickly, and I shut my eyes.

"Watch me," he said. "I want you to watch me come while I watch you come."

I opened my eyes and locked them with his.

Just in time, too, because the first spurts of come were jetting out of his cock, landing on his belly. Then more, some ending up on his thighs, and also his chest where it pooled for a moment, then ran down his chest in a stream.

My breathing was loud. I couldn't help it. I was so close.

"Come for me," he encouraged—*demanded*—again.

And I did as he said.

SEVEN

"You didn't think that was odd, did you?"

I looked at him. "No. It was…"

"It was what?"

I smiled. "It was hot as hell, is what it was."

We had cleaned up, got dressed, and were snuggling in a window seat together.

"You know," Max said, "we probably flew over your old neck of the woods while we were doing that."

It was an odd thought: flying over my old hometown, my parents down there somewhere, while I was thousands of feet in the air above them, having a mutual masturbation experience with a hot, rich guy who liked me.

I pinched his nipple through his shirt. "Don't make me think about that."

"Sorry," he said, laughing, and pushing my hand away. My head was on his chest and I loved hearing that deep rumble within him.

An hour later we landed at JFK airport. Max had arranged for a limo to be waiting for us, and soon we were in the heart of New York City. It was close to 2 a.m. local time, but to us it felt like only 11 p.m.

As we drove through the city, I looked out the window, trying to peer up at the huge buildings. LA isn't exactly a small town, but to me it was nothing like NYC. The streets were still fairly crowded with people. I figured most of them were going from one bar or club to another.

We got to the hotel, crashed, and I slept soundly until around nine the next morning. The only light in the room was soft and bluish, a thin ray streaming in through the window. From what I could see, it was cloudy, but not raining. I lay there for a few minutes just looking at Max. His shirt was off and the white sheet was bunched around his waist. He was on his back with one arm behind his head.

It's a bit much to call someone perfect, and I'm not naïve enough to think that of anyone. But this situation couldn't be more perfect. I was with a beautiful man who had a heart of gold. He had protected me when I could have been in danger that night when Chris showed up. He had whisked me off for an amazing weekend getaway in Napa, and now here we were in New York City, which promised to be just as amazing.

I thought about what we did on the plane. What a turn-on it was. How Max had done something so private in front of me, and how he had gotten me to do the same. I'd never let my walls down that much. Never shared something to intimate—so fucking hot!—with someone before.

When Max finally woke up, we lay there together on the cool sheets, with our bodies providing a soft warmth. I could have stayed like that all day, maybe all weekend, but Max was eager to get me out in the city and show me around.

We had brunch at an outside French café. We went to the Museum of Modern Art, walked past Radio City Music Hall, took a stroll through Central Park, and had a late lunch at a small Italian place, in the basement of a building, completely tourist free. It was just like the NYC Italian restaurants I'd seen in so many movies about mobsters. I didn't see anyone who looked suspiciously like they stepped off the set of *The Godfather* or *Goodfellas*. At one point I started to say something about that, but Max gave me a wide-eyed look that told me to wait until we were out of the place.

Later, back at the hotel, Max said he wanted to take me to a Broadway show.

"Seriously?" I think my voice went up an octave or two, making me sound like a kid who'd been promised something.

Max laughed. "Get dressed."

"I didn't bring anything nice."

He walked over to the armoire, opened the two doors, and showed me a gorgeous white dress.

"I ordered this for you yesterday."

"I was with you. How did you get it in here without me noticing?"

Max grabbed the hanger, removed the dress, and walked over to me. "I had them bring it up here. I'm just glad you weren't curious enough to look in there at some point."

"It's beautiful."

I leaned in to kiss him. "Come on. Let's take a quick shower and get dressed or we'll be late."

We had a hard time taking a quick shower together. Max lathered me up, spending quite a bit of unequal time on my breasts. I commented on it and he plead guilty.

I gave him the same treatment, only mine was probably more cruel: I had him hard as a rock by the time we were rinsing off.

"I want to fuck you right now," he said.

With my hand wrapped around his fully erect cock, I shook my head. "Later."

"Tease."

I was smiling as he kissed me. "If I tease you now, maybe we'll get back here later and you can fuck me senseless."

"You shouldn't challenge me," he said.

But he took the challenge, and held off. A part of me wanted him to pick me up, take me to the bed and do me hard and fast. But I was sure it would happen later.

The dress fit perfectly. With Max in his tux, we looked like we were going to dinner at the White House or Buckingham Palace.

The limo ride was short. Lucky for us. What little time we had in the car was spent teasing each other more. I almost suggested to Max that we skip the Broadway play and just ride around NYC, having sex in the limo. I don't know what got into me at some point in the day, but I was as horny as I could remember being in a long time.

The limo pulled to a stop. I hadn't even been looking around, so I didn't notice where Max was actually bringing me.

Hundreds of people were gathered beneath the marquee. Flashbulbs were going off like bursts of lightning. The path from the curb to the entrance of the building was a red carpet.

"Sorry," Max said. "I lied about the play."

I looked up at the marquee, saw the movie name, and in large letters: "PREMIER TONIGHT!"

Max took my hand in his. "I thought I'd surprise you by taking you to your first red carpet movie premier."

Wow. I'd had high hopes for seeing my first Broadway play, but this was even better.

Before I could process it all, the limo door was opened by a guy in a tux. Max stepped out, taking me by the hand and helping me out after him.

"Just keep up with me," he said, and started down the red carpet.

My eyes were flitting from left to right, looking at all the paparazzi and onlookers. They of course had no idea who I was, so all the camera flashes must have been for Max. But then I remembered he told me wasn't "that kind" of famous. He wasn't of great interest to the entertainment press. As successful as he was, he was known among them, but he was no Steven Spielberg or Quentin Tarantino in terms of fame in the public eye. And, from all that he'd confessed about being sick of the business, he was glad it was that way.

The frenzy of cameras wasn't as great as it was for the couple ahead of us and when I got inside I realized why. It was Nicole Kidman and Keith Urban. There were other stars milling around in the lobby, and Max introduced me to a few of them, including Kiefer Sutherland. I had to pretend that I knew what they were talking about when Max brought up something about the show *24*, but I'm not sure Mr. Sutherland cared either way.

Mostly, my head was buzzing as I scanned the lobby and spotted other famous people I'd only previously seen on TV. At one point, when I saw Morgan Freeman, I squeezed Max's hand so tightly he asked if I needed to use the bathroom or something.

"No!" I said, hitting his arm. And more quietly, I said, "Look who's over there."

"Olivia," Max said, without a hint of condescension in his voice, "if you're going to work in this business you're going to have to get used to seeing famous faces. In fact, it would do you some good to learn how to be cordial without letting them know you're impressed. Trust me."

He knew what he was talking about. He wouldn't have made it this far in the business if he didn't. Plus, I saw him put that advice into action the rest of the time we spend in the lobby drinking champagne and mingling. I stayed with Max the entire time. Or, more accurately, he tethered me to himself with a firm lock on my hand. I guess he didn't want me wandering off and making a fan-girl fool of myself. Again, he knew what he was doing.

"Do you know all these people?" I asked later, after the movie, as we attended the after-party in the grand lobby.

"Some."

"Even the ones you haven't worked with."

He sipped from his White Russian. "You meet people lots of different ways. By the way, I'd like to compliment you on leaving your phone in your purse all night. That shows a lot of self-control."

I squinted my eyes at him. "Maybe I'll whip it out now and start snapping pictures."

Max leaned toward me, his lips against my ear. "Maybe I'll whip something else out and fuck you right here."

He pulled away, keeping eye contact with me, and taking another sip of his drink.

I took a few steps toward the middle of the room. "How about right here?"

Max's hand went to his belt buckle. "If you say so…"

I burst out laughing. A little too loud, it turns out, because I attracted the attention of a few people around us. Luckily it was no one famous. I stepped toward Max and threw my arms around his neck. "Will you *please* take me back to our room and fuck me?"

EIGHT

"I thought you said elevator sex was cliché."

"This isn't sex," Max said. "And I can't resist you, so cliché or not, we're going to do this."

I had my back against the wall of the hotel's elevator car. Max had both hands against the wall, over my shoulders, caging me.

"Touch me," he said.

My palm glided down the front of his shirt. I felt his hard chest and stomach beneath my hand.

My heart started beating faster as my hand reached his belt buckle. It was still fastened and I wondered if I should undo it, but as I explored a little farther, I realized that he had simply unzipped.

His erection was pointing upward a little, as if waiting to greet me.

I felt the soft, fleshy head of it. First with my palm. Then I closed a few fingertips around it. The tip was wet. Max was extremely turned on.

He was sucking on one of my nipples as I touched him and he said, “That feels amazing,” through a breathy sigh. “ What are you thinking?” he asked.

I had to remember to breathe. I kept holding my breath, not even aware of it. I took in some air and said, “I can’t believe what I’m doing.”

“Holding a big cock in your hand?”

“More than that,” I said.

“Standing here with your tits out, getting your nipples sucked?”

His hot talk was turning me on. Hearing him describe what we were doing in such a blunt way got me even more excited. I said, “You’re so hard.”

“Because of you.”

He kissed me fully, our hot and wet mouths meeting, our tongues sliding along each other’s with incredible passion.

I took him into my hand, trying to wrap my fingers around his hard-on as much as I could. He was long and thick. I stroked him from the base, up the length of his shaft, to the tip, then back down again. He was as hard as I could imagine a guy getting. The skin was warm and soft, almost velvety, especially around the tip.

A drop of semen gathered at the tip and it got on my hand, serving as a lubricant as I stroked him.

"We should leave," I said, as reality and logic suddenly snapped me out of the haze I'd been in for the last several minutes.

"No," he said. "Not yet."

"What?" I was baffled at the risk he was willing to take. "They're going to find us here. Someone is."

"That makes it better, doesn't it? Besides, I haven't felt all of you yet."

"Max, I'm serious."

"I know you are," he said. "You're also wet."

I was. I could feel it. I was wet and hot and my inner thighs were almost tingling.

He started kissing my neck, one of my weaknesses. I was very aroused and it was made more vivid by the risk we were taking and by the fear of getting caught in the elevator.

I felt Max's cock getting harder as I stroked him faster. I felt it pulsating in my hand. I felt it pumping. Then I felt his hot come on my thigh, running down my leg.

When he started to spurt he pulled his hand out of my underwear and put it on the wall, so both hands were on either side of my head. He leaned on the wall as he had his orgasm. He moved his hips back and forth, as though he were fucking my hand, and then I felt his semen spurting out and then more, and more.

"Fuck," he said through a heavy breath.

I was totally embarrassed. Which is what I knew he wanted. When he finally did finish, he moved back a little, put his cock back into his pants and zipped up.

"That was incredible," he said. "I think there's some on your dress."

Oh no. Stupidly, or perhaps just because of the circumstances, I hadn't even thought of that. "I need to see it in the light," I said, frantically situating my dress back over my breasts. As I straightened the lower part of my dress, I felt it for sure. Splashes of his semen on my dress, rivulets of it succumbing to gravity and making its way down to my legs.

Max took his pocket-square out of his jacket and wiped it up as best he could.

"When we get to the room, I'm afraid you'll have to take this dress off so we can let this spot soak."

I smiled. "How convenient."

"This could get complicated," Max said, sliding the card into the lock when we got to his hotel room.

"How so?"

He took a deep breath. "Complicated in the sense of..." His voice trailed off. "Well, let me put it this way. Can you stop?"

"Stop what?"

"Stop what we're doing," he said. "If I told you in the next ten seconds that we would never again do what we've been doing, the way we've been doing it, would you be okay with that?"

I had to think about it for a minute.

The silence prompted him to speak. "I think the answer is no."

I said, "What makes you say that?"

"The pause."

"That pause could have been me figuring out a way to tell you I do want to stop," I said.

Max laughed. "I don't think so, honey."

There was a cockiness in his tone. Normally I'd be the first to roll my eyes and dismiss a guy who was so sure of himself. But Max was different in so many ways.

He continued, "I think you'd start it up on your own if I stopped."

Dammit. He was probably right. I didn't want to admit it, though.

He said, "Can you go back to life before me?"

"I can live without it," I said, taunting him.

This time it was Max who paused before saying, "I'm sure you could live without me. But the question is: Would you *want* to?"

That was indeed the question, and the answer was no.

When I told him, he took my hand and led me to the bedroom.

Max said: "All afternoon I've been thinking about how I couldn't wait to get you naked and make you come all over my cock."

He hadn't done this much dirty talking since I met him, and it was beginning to have a strangely intoxicating effect on me.

He lowered the zipper on my dress, quickly shoved it down my body, and I stepped out of it. I was standing there with my back to him, wearing only a bra, panty-hose and shoes.

The shoes didn't last long. Neither did the hose. Max removed them and, still with my back to him, he finished undressing me.

Last to go was the bra. His hands went for it, and in seconds it too was on the floor. I was completely naked.

"Turn around," he said.

I was turning, but apparently not fast enough for him because he helped spin me around. The next thing I knew I was on my back on the bed.

Max was hovering over me, licking my nipples. I watched his mouth as he clamped onto each nipple, trading off, back and forth, taking each one fully into his mouth.

He kissed the area between my breasts and then started down my stomach and finally stopping right as his mouth made contact with my clitoris.

I felt his tongue flicking on it.

I put my hands on his head.

I was squirming a lot and Max said, "Do you want to come like this?"

"Yes. Yes..." I could barely get the words out.

"Maybe later," he teased.

Without saying anything, he stood up, reached out for my hand and I took it. He pulled me to a sitting position, stood in front of me, fully clothed. He even still had his jacket on.

Still silent, not warning me at all, his hands went to his pants zipper, and all of a sudden I was sitting there and Max was holding his fully erect cock right in front of my face.

He gave it a few strokes. I couldn't take my eyes off of it.

"I want to see what you look like with a cock in your mouth," he said.

I closed my eyes and leaned forward, my lips pursed tightly. I kissed the tip of his cock and felt that slick fluid sticking to my lips.

"Put your hand down," he said, and I dropped the hand that was holding it in place.

He started moving his hips back and forth. I moved away when he thrust forward because the first time he did that it went in too deep.

He brushed the hair away from my face. I opened my eyes, looked up at his, and saw him craning his neck to the side a little so he had a full view of himself sliding in and out of my mouth.

"You look amazing," he said. "So hot. I love fucking your mouth."

I felt the veined ridges of his erection on my lips. I felt how much bigger the tip was when he squeezed and made it bulge even more.

He was starting to throb more and more, and frequently. At once, I wanted him to come in my mouth, but I also didn't want any of this to end.

He pulled it out of my mouth, put his hand on his erection and gave it a few light strokes. I tried to get my jaw to relax. It felt like it was cramping.

Max put his hand on my shoulder, directed me onto my back. "Move back more," he said.

As I moved farther back on the bed, he stripped naked. I watched him take his clothes off and drank in his tight, hard athlete's body as though it were the first time I was seeing it. As he stood there naked for a few seconds, I again looked down and saw his hardness. I was only seconds away from having it inside me.

Max knelt before me and stroked himself with one hand, his other hand between my legs, rubbing me up and down.

"You look so hot," he said. "I have to taste you again."

He lowered his head between my legs.

"Touch yourself," he commanded.

I moved my hands up and down my legs, going closer to my pussy with each pass, finally getting my fingers in place. I spread myself open, giving him a close-up view of my excited clit.

"Beautiful," he said. "Show me how you do it."

I circled the pad of my forefinger around. He told me to stick my finger out, and when I did he took it into his mouth, sucked on it, then pulled away, leaving my finger dripping with his saliva.

I circled my clit a little faster, then slipped one finger into my hole, joined a second later by another.

"I love watching you finger yourself."

I looked down and saw how close his face was. Inwardly I was begging him to lick me, but I couldn't ask for it. I'd have to wait until he was ready.

Which didn't take long.

His head lowered again and he turned it a little to one side, pushing my hand away. "All mine."

He slipped a finger into me, turned it up a little, massaging my soft inner walls.

And his tongue had stopped teasing—it was now right where I'd been dying to feel it.

I positioned myself up on my elbows a little so I could look farther down and have a clear view of what he was doing to me. He moved both of his arms under me to lift my pelvis up. I had a perfect line of sight now and watched his every movement.

"You like watching?" he said, between licks, and looking up to make eye contact.

I nodded.

"Tell me."

I took a breath and said, "I love watching you bathe me with your tongue."

"Nice, Olivia. Very dirty."

His fingers parted me. His tongue swirled around my clit, like he was polishing a fine pearl.

His finger moved a little faster, now making circles inside, matching the rhythmic movement of his tongue.

I said, "Do it, right there, oh yeah…"

"Ask."

"Please," I said, having momentarily forgotten my role.

He started flicking his tongue up and down on my clit, just the end of his tongue making contact with me, trying to heighten the sensitivity, and tease it a little.

My hips were moving up and down.

He slid one finger into me, and he asked me if I wanted two. I said yes, and felt them go in a little tightly, but I was slick and soon each finger was buried in me.

Then a third entered me. But not where I expected. Without warning, he had turned his hand to face down, two fingers in my pussy, and his thumb had entered my ass.

I felt the warm walls of my pussy twitch and tighten, then relax, then tighten again. A perfect rhythm started, and my legs closed around his head.

I was coming....

"Oh yeah, yeah, yeah..." Over and over I said it, unable to stop.

Moments later, he leaned down over me and kissed my lips, feeding me my own taste.

Then he went for my neck, then lower, and started sucking on my nipples again. I felt his erection on me now, between my legs, just outside of me. He lowered himself and started sliding his cock around on my pussy—my wetness mixing with his.

"Max."

He looked deeply into my eyes.

I said, "Don't use a condom." We had discussed the fact that I was taking birth control, but still played it safe…until now.

"Are you sure?"

"Yes. Do it. Just do it."

"I love when you beg me."

Without warning, he slid into me. I gasped. He was stretching me as he pushed in, farther, deeper, slowly at first and then he plunged it all the way in. I felt his balls against my butt—that's how close we were, with him all the way inside of me.

He pulled out, not all the way but a long stroke retreating from me. Then, back in, this time faster and just as deep. There was a little pain that went along with it. Not much, but just enough on the edge of the pleasure I also felt.

He sat straight up, his cock deep within me, looked down at me and started rocking his hips back and forth.

"You feel so fuckin' good," he said. He looked down. "I wish you could see this."

All I could do was breathe heavily. I didn't have anything to say. I also didn't want him to stop.

"Do you love my cock?"

"Yessss."

"Say it."

"I love your cock."

"Tell me you love my cock fucking your tight cunt."

"I love your big cock in my cunt."

I felt Max's erection twitch, then pulsate more, twitch again and then he said, "Fuck, I'm gonna come, Olivia." He had been lying right on top of me after my orgasm and he was really going at it.

I had my hands above my head on the bed by this point. He went back to the sitting position and I watched as he looked down at himself going in and out....

Then I felt his hot semen spurting, filling me. Max trembled as he pumped his orgasm into me—shot after shot, like he would never stop coming.

But when he finally did, he collapsed on top of me, and I loved the heavy, hot, sweaty weight of him on me.

We didn't talk for a few minutes. I still had no idea what to say and he was trying to catch his breath.

I don't know where it came from. Maybe just unfiltered honesty. Making myself emotionally vulnerable to him, now that I'd made myself physically his. Regardless, what came out of my mouth was: "This is the most amazing thing that's ever happened to me."

Max rolled onto his side and pulled me close to his warm body.

"Wait 'til you see what comes next."

NINE

Sunday evening, back in LA, I entered my apartment to find it empty once again. Krystal was hardly ever there. If it weren't for Max, I would have felt pretty lonely much of the time. That, or I'd have to go out and make friends, which never came easily to me unless someone else did the introducing.

I did my weekly check-in with my parents. Mom said Dad had been sick all week with some kind of stomach bug and was sleeping so I didn't get to talk with him.

We talked about my week, and I made up a lie about my weekend. I told her I'd been resting and watching TV and cleaning the apartment. The boring nature of the lie was deliberate, so as not to spark any questions from her. Something as simple as saying I went to dinner and a movie would leave me having to remember more false statements.

Then she said, "Your father and I have been talking about taking a trip out there to see you. Just for a few days."

I didn't see that coming. I was silent for a few seconds and said, "Really?"

"Well, don't sound so excited about it."

"Sorry."

"If you don't want us to come..."

"No, Mom, it's not that. It's just a surprise, that's all."

Surprise was actually a mild word for what I was feeling. I hadn't even considered the idea that they'd come all the way out here to visit. We'd never discussed it, and they weren't much for traveling. On top of that, I immediately wondered how I would handle the whole thing with Max. I hadn't mentioned a word to them about him, and to do so now, as they prepared to come for a visit, would look more like a confession rather than a happy announcement that I had a boyfriend. For now, I decided I should keep quiet about it and figure it out later.

"Well, would that be okay with you?" she asked.

"Of course it would. When were you thinking about taking the trip?"

"Maybe at the end of the month," she said.

"Is Grace coming?"

"We haven't talked to her about it yet."

I really hoped my sister would come. I wanted to see the baby, for one thing, but also having Grace around would lessen the intense parental pressure I'd feel. No doubt there would be an inquisition about my living arrangements and my entire new life in LA.

Mom said we could talk more about it next week when I called. I told her to pass along a "Get well" message to Dad, and we ended the call.

I was exhausted but also craving a snack, so I filled a small bowl with fresh blueberries and settled down on the couch to flip through the channels and wind down a bit. When the TV came on, there was a still picture on it. I couldn't tell what it was and thought the cable was out and had frozen on a channel, but it turned out the DVD was on and paused.

I pushed PLAY on the remote, then found myself sitting there with two blueberries in my mouth, unable to chew, shocked by what I was watching.

It was Krystal having sex with two guys.

I probably should have hit STOP, or maybe even dropped the bowl of fruit and run out of the room in total astonishment. But the truth is, I couldn't stop looking.

Krystal was naked, except for a gold chain around her waist that attached to her belly-button ring. She was on all fours, her ass just off the edge of the bed. One guy stood behind her, fucking her, while another guy knelt in front of her as she sucked his cock.

It didn't dawn on me at first, but this wasn't simply Krystal and two guys taping themselves having sex. Someone was operating the camera. The video also switched from different angles and skipped ahead to different scenes—Krystal on her back with one guy fucking her, another guy kneeling just behind her head with his cock over her face while she licked and sucked him; Krystal riding a guy reverse cowgirl style, with the other guy standing on the bed with his cock in her mouth; and the finale: Krystal on top of one of the guys and the other one behind her, fucking her in the ass.

I've always had a nosey, curious side to me, but this was probably the worst example of lack of self-control on my part. I wish I hadn't watched the entire fifteen minutes, but I did.

My earlier suspicions about Krystal having a waitressing job were confirmed. She was doing porn for a living. No wonder she never asked me to help her get representation from an agent. What kind of aspiring actress would have a roommate who worked for a Hollywood agent, and never once float the possibility of using that connection to get her foot in the door?

It wasn't my place to judge her, but I was sure I wouldn't be able to look at her the same way for a while.

I jolted upright off the couch, realizing that if she walked in, she'd find me looking at the DVD. I didn't want her to know, didn't want that kind of awkwardness. I grabbed the remote and ran the DVD back to the point where I thought she had paused it before. I turned off the TV and went to my room to try to get some sleep.

But it wouldn't happen. My mind was racing. I had to tell someone. I couldn't tell Grace. For one thing, it was almost 2 a.m. back in Ohio. Plus, I couldn't be so sure that she wouldn't freak out, blurt it out to my parents, and then I'd have to deal with a ration of shit about living in Hollywood with someone who does porn. No doubt my parents would project that on me and think I'd gone down a one-way street to Hell.

I called Max, who answered almost immediately. "Everything okay?"

"Fine. Why?"

"Just making sure you didn't have any unwanted visitors."

I sighed. "Let's not bring him up anymore. I told you, he's back in Ohio."

"He better stay there."

"I have something pretty wild to tell you."

When I finished telling Max about the DVD, he said, "Typical."

"Huh?"

"It happens to a lot of girls who come here looking for stardom. They end up in low-budget porn. I've seen it happen a thousand times."

I said, "Really?"

"Don't get any ideas."

I laughed. "Uh, you don't have to worry about that. I'd never do that. Besides, I'm having the best sex of my life right now."

"*Right now*? Who's there?"

"Shut up, you know what I mean."

"Yeah, I do. And anyway, you're not breathless like you usually are when you're doing it." He chuckled, and then there was silence, which wasn't exactly what I wanted to hear. I had hoped he would agree and tell me that he was having the best sex of his life, too. But he didn't say it.

It was a good thing that I didn't confess to the other feeling I had developed. I was falling in love with him.

TEN

I'm standing with my back to the wall, and he has me trapped. He's backlit, and all I can see is his silhouette, standing about two feet in front of me. I have no escape. My body shakes with fear. Adrenaline is coursing through my veins. I could try to run, but I know he'd catch me. I see the silhouette's right shoulder dip and pull back. Then the most frightening thing I'd ever seen: he has made a fist and he's cocking his arm back for the punch, level with my face.

I awoke from the dream in a cold sweat. I was drenched, and so were the sheets. I was shaking. Scared. My heart was racing. My mouth felt as dry as cotton.

It was the same dream I'd had about Chris many times. It never varied. It was always one-hundred percent factual, almost not like a dream at all, but a memory burned into my subconscious emerging every once in a while to haunt me.

But this time there was a difference. Not in the setting. Not in the lighting. Not in the order of events. This time, the person raising his fist was Max.

What the fuck did that mean?

The clock read 3:38 a.m. There is no more lonely place than the middle of the night when you're awake, by yourself and scared, sad or both.

I got out of the bed, ripped the sheets off and tossed them to the floor. At some point I had pushed the comforter away, so it had escaped the sweat. I pulled the t-shirt over my head, slipped out of my panties, tossed them in the hamper and went to the bathroom where I toweled off my damp body. I got back on the bed—on the harshly uncomfortable bare mattress—and covered myself with the comforter as I shivered.

Somehow I managed to fall back asleep after about thirty minutes of being afraid to let myself fall into that dream again.

Why Max? Why had my brain allowed that to happen?

6:45 a.m., the alarm woke me. Thank God I hadn't had a continuation of that terrifying dream. It still lingered, though, and I thought about it way too much as I showered and prepared for the day.

By the time I left my room and made my way to the kitchen to get some juice and fruit, Krystal was just coming in the door. She looked awful. Her hair was ragged. Her skin was an ashy pale color. She had bags under her eyes. She looked like she had aged fifteen years.

"Are you okay?" I asked.

She yawned and said, "Fine, yeah, why?"

"Just making sure." I could barely even look at her. Not just because of her appearance but also because her porn video was running on a loop in my mind.

On the way into work, I didn't play any music. I spent the entire time trying to process why I might have had that awful dream about Max.

He had never done anything to make me feel the least bit threatened.

Physically, anyway....

Maybe the violence in the dream was a manifestation of my being afraid of him hurting me in some other way. The entire time we had been seeing each other, I'd been having those lingering thoughts that I wasn't cut out to be with someone like Max.

Later, at lunch, we talked on the phone but I didn't dare tell him about the dream. It would have opened up all kinds of possibilities for conflict, and I didn't want to do that. After all,

I'd pretty much figured out the source of the dream, so why burden him with an issue I needed to get over myself?

Not to mention our conversation was going so well. He told me he had a great time in NYC and I told him it was amazing.

"But," I said, "maybe this weekend we keep our feet on the ground."

"Does that rule out me carrying you to my bed?"

"I'd never rule that out. You know that."

"Okay, so we stay in town. But I want you to myself all weekend. No going out. I'll cook, we'll talk, watch movies..." His voice trailed off.

"And?"

"And what?"

"That's it?" I said playfully, and I knew he could probably hear the smile in my voice.

"Some things go without saying," he replied.

I didn't say anything. Just thinking about what we'd done in that hotel room on Saturday night, and Max's comment about me waiting to see what comes next...well, it just had me vocally paralyzed.

I avoided Krystal all day and the next, which wasn't difficult. She wasn't around that much. I heard her coming and going late at night, but never saw her because I was in my room most of the time.

Max called me early Wednesday morning and said he was going to have to cancel our dinner plans. I was disappointed, but figured it might be best. For one thing, I kind of liked the idea of the anticipation building. On top of that, he was becoming something of a distraction, consuming all of my thoughts that didn't have to do with work. Actually, he was consuming some of those, too, whenever I talked to Jacqueline Mathers, who was turning out to be a pain-in-the-ass client.

She called me twice on Monday. The first call was to find out if I thought she would be asked to do the late-night talk shows, and if so, could I make sure he was booked for Letterman? "If I'm going to get on Howard Stern's show, I better not go on Leno."

"Why's that?"

"Because Howard hates Leno!"

Apparently she thought she was on a first-name basis with Howard Stern. She filled me in on the feud, and I did all I could not to nod off during the boring story.

I told her I wasn't sure it was time yet to think about booking appearances, and when the time did come, we'd have to ask Kevin about the Howard Stern idea.

"But you think Letterman's a possibility?"

I really had no idea, but I said, "Sure. Of course."

The second time she called, later that afternoon, she asked me if she'd have a driver to the studio and various set locations when shooting started.

I talked to Kevin, who told me: "Get used to it. They get one film and they think they're the hottest thing in town. And for our sake, we better hope she is. Tell her we'll make it happen." He shut his laptop and shook his head. "Jesus."

I felt better now that I knew Kevin had the same thoughts I was having about Jacqueline.

ELEVEN

I stopped at a Starbucks on Friday morning on my way in to work. There was a bounce in my step and a flutter in my chest. I was thinking "TGIF" not just because the weekend was coming, but because I would be spending the entire weekend with Max.

In the shower earlier, I thought about what it would be like to live with him. I imagined myself as the wife of this incredible man—not just professionally, but personally as well. I thought of the great sex we'd already had and would have much more of over the weekend. I had mental images and matching warm feelings of comfort thinking about how safe and desired I felt when he held me in his arms.

I'd had all week to get that stupid dream out of my head. More to the point, I had all week to work through my self-limiting fears of whether I was worthy or not. Of course I was. I wasn't going to let anyone tell me I wasn't, least of all myself.

When I got to work, Kevin was waiting in my office. That had never happened before. I looked at my watch to make sure I wasn't late, and sure enough I wasn't.

I walked in and he said, "Have a seat," as though I had walked into *his* office. His voice was flat and he sounded concerned. He had his iPad in his lap.

I sat down and said, "What's going on?"

"Olivia, can you explain this?"

He held up the iPad. I looked at the screen and saw a picture of Max and me on the red carpet at the movie premier in New York. Well, it wasn't exactly a picture of us—it was a picture of Gwenyth Paltrow, and Max and I were in the background. The photo was snapped just as Max and I were emerging from the limo.

Damn. If only the background had been just a little more out of focus, I wouldn't have been sitting there facing this inquiry.

I decided to be quick and blunt with the truth. Why run from it?

"I went to New York with him over the weekend."

"When did this come about?"

"It started a few weeks ago."

He sighed and looked at the picture again.

"I don't have to tell you how bad this could be," he said. "Do I?"

I shook my head. I knew all the ramifications of this for Kevin professionally, and by extension for me as well. I had thought it through early on when things started with Max. But in the meantime, my only concern had become for me personally, and the emotional wreckage that I might become if I let myself get too close to him. Too late. I was already there, and there was no going back.

Kevin continued: "Look, I understand if you got swept off your feet by Max Dalton. But you should have at least told me you were seeing him. This could complicate our working relationship."

I wondered if he meant his working relationship with Max, or with me. Was he thinking of firing me? No, that would be a stupid move. He'd just landed his biggest deal with a major Hollywood producer, so how could he possibly fire his assistant who was dating that major Hollywood producer? The notion was fraught with career suicide for Kevin. And it was all just dawning on me. So I relaxed.

I didn't say anything, though. I just let him finish. "Be careful."

I hoped the ominous tone in his voice was unintended. The warning sounded like something more than an admonition to play things safe for the sake of his agency.

"Careful?" I asked.

Kevin looked down at his iPad without saying anything. He touched the screen a couple of times, scrolled down, then turned it so the screen was facing me.

I was looking at a tabloid website. There was a large photo of Max with a tall blonde woman under the snarky and typically unprofessional headline: "SOAP STAR'S BABY DADDY".

Holy shit.

I read the first two paragraphs of the story. The woman was a soap opera actress named Liza Carrow. Rumors had been swirling for weeks, apparently, about her being pregnant and how they would work it into the show. And, as always happens in celebrity news, the major question was about who the father was.

The photo was taken two days ago outside a Thai restaurant in Los Angeles. The story named Max and told readers who he was, but the focus of it was really Liza Carrow. At least, that's how the tabloid had intended it.

For me, the focus was Max.

It's not often that you can shoo your boss out of your office, but that's pretty much what I did. "I need to be by myself."

That's all I had to say. Kevin got up and left.

I sat there for a few minutes, stunned. Then started feeling stupid for letting myself get into this so deeply. I *knew* I shouldn't have. My instincts were right.

My cell phone rang. I got it out of my purse and looked at the screen. It was Max, of course, no doubt calling me about the story that had been broken by the tabloid. I let it ring three times, and then decided I needed to hear his voice. I needed to hear his explanation. Avoiding him wouldn't do any good.

"Hello," I said, flatly.

"Olivia. I need to see you."

I stayed silent for a moment and then decided to play along. "Is something wrong?"

"We need to talk. In person."

"Max, what is it?" I said, pulling off the fake surprise and worry pretty nicely, I thought.

He sighed, but didn't say anything.

A part of me wanted to scream at him—scream that he had betrayed me, lied to me, kept something hugely important from me, as we spent more and more time together, and all the while he *knew* I was feeling closer to him. Bastard.

"I'm coming to pick you up," he said.

"When?"

"Right now."

My throat was starting to tighten up as I held back from crying. "I…I'm working."

"I need to see you, Olivia. It can't wait. I'm pulling into the parking lot now."

He hung up. Fuck.

I immediately grabbed my purse, stopped by Kevin's office and started to tell him what was going on. He was looking out his office window. "Go do what you need to do. Take the rest of the day off." There was sympathy in his voice. I knew he was being genuine.

"Thanks. And I'm sorry."

Kevin just shook his head. "Go."

I turned to leave the office and thought about Kevin's phrase: "…do what you need to do." Hell, I didn't know what I needed to do. I didn't know what I wanted to do, either. What I really wanted was for none of this to happen. I wished I had never gotten involved with Max. Wished I had never trusted him. Wished I had never let my feelings for him grow.

When I got outside, he was standing next to my car.

"Get out of my way," I said.

He didn't move. "So you know."

"Of course I know. And you want to know how? My fucking boss saw a fucking picture of us in fucking New York, then he showed me the picture of you and your pregnant…girlfriend or fuck-buddy or whatever she is."

"Olivia, calm d—"

"No! You don't get to tell me to calm down. You don't get to tell me anything ever again."

I pushed at him, moving him out of my way so I could get into my car.

"Jesus, Olivia. Let me explain!"

I didn't respond. I closed the car door, locked it, put the key in the ignition, threw the car into reverse, and tore out of there as fast as I could.

Fuck him and his lies, I thought.

TWELVE

I was so glad it was Friday and I had the whole weekend to stay in the apartment and not have to go anywhere. This was supposed to be a romantic stay-inside weekend alone with Max, and now it had turned into a stay-inside lonely pity party. Amazing how things can change in the blink of an eye.

I was pretty sure I'd have the place to myself. It was the weekend and Krystal would be off doing…whatever it was that she does. And, frankly, I didn't care.

I didn't sleep much. I spent a lot of time lying on my bed, looking up at the ceiling, wondering how much worse my trust issues would be after Max. They were already so damaged before he came into my life, and now he would be leaving my life, a path of emotional destruction in his wake.

I don't even think I could have sorted out how much of my feelings were from anger and how much came from sadness. It was all a horrible blend.

I turned my phone off when I got home and left it off until Saturday afternoon. I expected Max to be knocking on my door, but that never materialized. Maybe he'd just given up altogether. Maybe it would be better that way.

Saturday morning, I did a Google search for Liza Carrow. She was an up-and-coming star in the soap opera world. I never watched them so I had no idea who she was at first. Her IMDb page listed no other credits. But there were lots of photos, and she was stunningly gorgeous. My heart wrenched when I thought of Max on top of her, fucking her the same way he did me, or her on top, riding him.

She was four months pregnant, so there was a possibility that Max hadn't slept with her since that time, well before we met. I'd have no way of knowing, no matter what he said. Was he with her in public simply because he was the father? Or was he still sleeping with her?

I could find no other stories from the rumor mills pointing to anyone else as the father.

I wanted to vomit, but luckily I hadn't eaten anything all day.

I closed my laptop and lay on the bed, once again staring up at the ceiling. I needed to close my eyes and go to sleep, but any hope of nodding off into escapism vanished when there was a knock at my bedroom door.

"Olivia?"

It was Krystal's voice.

"Yeah?"

"Can I come in?"

Shit. *No, I need to be alone right now.* That's what I should have said, but I'm not sure it would have made a bit of difference. When I didn't answer, she said there was something she needed to give me.

I got up and opened the door. Krystal stood there looking rested and nicely dressed. I hadn't been expecting that. She handed me a large manila envelope with my name on it. "This was on the front porch."

My name was definitely written in Max's handwriting.

"Thanks," I said.

"Are you okay?"

"Yeah, I'm fine. Let me see what this is."

"Okay, well I'm getting ready to leave, so I'll see you later."

I closed the door and went back to the bed. The envelope was thick and heavy. Did I want to open this right now? Not really, I thought, but I just had to look.

I opened it and pulled out what looked to be a movie script—typed, and fastened with the two brackets, as they always are.

Attached to the cover page was a note:

Olivia – Please read this. I wrote this script when I was 22, but the movie was never made. I never thought I'd meet anyone who was anything like the female lead character I made up for this script. Then I met you. Read it and you'll understand.

You should let me explain everything that happened this week.

I'm not going to give up easily.

I hope you won't, either. -Max

I spent the next two hours reading the script. I'd never read one before, so it was my first experience with reading something in that format. So much of it was dialogue, brilliant dialogue. It was a beautiful love story—a guy who is starting to feel lost in life, a girl who comes along and shows him that while there's plenty to be cynical about, she is not among those things. She's real. She's genuine. She's not corrupted by the world that the guy is so used to.

Near the beginning of the script, there's paragraph explaining the female lead's motivation, and in Max's handwriting were the words: Manic Pixie Dream Girl. I wondered what that meant, so I Googled it and smiled when I discovered that it was a term used to describe the female lead in one of my favorite movies: *Elizabethtown.*

I loved that story and I loved the character played by Kirsten Dunst. I remember the first time I saw it, thinking it was the quirkiest and most romantic movie I could remember seeing. It was all real-life situations, but it truly was a fairy-tale love story and a story about a man finding out who he really is…with the help of a girl who appeared out of nowhere just at the right time.

When I got to the end of the script there was a note from Max, directing me back to that paragraph, just in case I had missed it. He wrote:

You'll see why I never made this movie. Someone had already done one like it. But this remains my favorite thing I've ever written. You're the only person on the planet who has seen it. – M

As much as I loved and admired her, I really had never thought of myself as anything like the character in *Elizabethtown*. But maybe to Max, that's exactly who I was.

His dream girl.

That's what he was telling me.

Shit. I had retreated too quickly. I hadn't given him a chance to explain. Maybe there was nothing to the story. Maybe it was just another tabloid piece of junk journalism.

I felt so stupid. I at least owed it to Max to let him explain. I just had to.

I scrounged around for my phone, turned it on, and dialed his number. I waited through three rings….

….and then he answered: "Hello, dream girl."

FADE INTO ALWAYS

ONE

Max called me a "dream girl."

What was I supposed to say after that? Nothing, I hope, because I couldn't have said anything at that moment even if I'd wanted to. There was no buildup to the crying outburst. It just happened suddenly.

Through my sobs I could hear him saying, "Let me come get you."

I managed to say "Okay," and he told me he was on his way.

I went to see if Krystal was around, to let her know Max was coming over and I was glad to find that she had gone out. I really wanted the place to myself rather than being locked up in my bedroom.

What was I going to say to him? What was he going to say to me? My mind raced with the possibilities. Should I tell him I was falling in love with him? Was it too much too soon, and would it scare him off?

I sat on the couch and flipped through the screenplay again. Reading the two main characters' dialogue was like listening to them. That's how good a writer Max was. And I could really understand why he loved it so much. He was born to do this.

There were some scenes throughout the writing that made me wonder if they were based on actual events or conversations, or if he'd made them up. If they were real, my heart would break for him. Even if they weren't, they had still come from his mind, and so somewhere deep in his psyche—or maybe not so deep—resided all this pain. But also an intense desire to douse the flames of his past and move on to something just as beautiful as he'd conjured up on the page.

For a split second I thought it might be Krystal at the door, but then I remembered giving Max a key several days ago. He'd refused at first, saying he felt like it breached some kind of personal space that I was entitled to, and that he'd never just come and go as he pleased, but I told him that's what I wanted.

The door opened and as he was turning to close it, I stood from the couch and made my way over to him. Probably too quickly. Too *eagerly* is more like it.

Max turned and took me in his arms. He tried to just hug me, but I forced my face to his and took his mouth hungrily. He met my advances with equal enthusiasm, and we stood there kissing for what must have been two minutes.

When things slowed down he said, "Let's sit. I want to tell you everything."

I shook my head. "No. Not now."

I grabbed his hand and started heading for the steps, up to my bedroom, where I closed the door behind us, stepped toward Max and pushed his chest, sending him falling backward onto the bed.

"No talking," I said, climbing up on the bed and straddling him.

I pulled his shirt up, revealing his stomach and chest, and licked—from his abs, upward, running my tongue around each of his nipples.

I slid one hand behind his back and beneath his belt, into his pants, cupping his ass.

If he had any trouble with me taking such forceful charge, he wasn't showing the slightest bit of a clue.

I wanted to ravish him. Take him as mine. Have him the way he'd had me so many times.

Pressing myself into him, I felt him getting hard—my panties and his jeans were barriers, but still I felt the full effect of what I was doing to him. And as long as he kept letting me have my way with him, it wouldn't be long until there was nothing between us....

"These need to come off," I said, sitting up and unbuckling his belt. I moved off the bed, pulled his shoes off and yanked his pants down—along with his boxers. He was fully hard and I wasted no time moving back on top of him, pulling my panties off just before straddling him again.

I pressed my mouth to his and my tongue dove into his mouth. I rocked my hips, my wet pussy sliding along his rigid length. I got into a rhythm that could easily have made me come, and I kept going. Teasing him, gliding my warmth back and forth on him.

I sat up and pulled my shirt over my head, then unhooked my bra and tossed it aside. I leaned over his face, my breasts there for him to take.

And he did. Max's tongue touched one of my nipples and a shiver of excitement zapped through my body.

Max was sucking on my nipples, hard, switching back and forth. He pressed into my breast and I watched as my flesh enveloped his face. Sometimes I hated having big boobs, but the way Max responded to them made all the annoyances somehow worth it.

He dropped his head back on the pillow. "I can't wait anymore."

I wanted to tease him longer, but the truth was that I couldn't wait anymore either.

I slid along his cock until I felt the head notch against my opening. Max felt it, too, and moved his hips, pushing the head into me as I eased back and let it slide in.

"Fuck, Olivia," Max hissed.

"That's what you're doing," I said. "You're fucking Olivia."

My words caused him to thrust upward, his cock inside me to the hilt. I gyrated my hips around in circles, taking him in as deep and snug as I could get him.

I loved driving him crazy. Watching the way his eyes narrowed. The way he breathed with an open mouth. The way his nostrils flared. The way he arched his back and tilted his head back as he drove into me from below.

I sat straight up and felt him as deep as I'd ever felt him.

Max reached up with both hands and cupped my breasts in his hands, then tweaked my nipples simultaneously with his thumbs and fingertips.

I rocked back and forth on him, then moved my legs so I was squatting over him. Max put his hands under my thighs to give me some support…and I started bouncing on his cock.

He looked down his body and watched me slide up and down on it. Watched himself disappearing inside me. Watch me taking his long shaft deep into my body.

He was gritting his teeth, and bearing them—animalistic—and I loved seeing the effect I was having on him.

"Slow down," he said hoarsely.

"You gonna come?"

"Yes. Slow down," he said, his voice deeper, commanding.

But I didn't take his order. "You can't make me. It's my turn to control you. Just this once…"

And with that he threw his head back onto the pillow, thrust his hips up forcefully, and held them there.

I felt his semen pumping into me. The hot slickness making my bouncing feel even better for me, and I felt the first quiver inside.

"Oh yeah," he groaned, feeling me clenching and milking him. "Come for me."

"I'm coming…"

TWO

"Jump in and ask me anything you want," Max said. "But let me start talking."

We were in the kitchen, sitting at the table, eating apple slices, and cheese on sesame crackers. It was pretty much all I had there, but it was a great late-night snack. Max, as usual, was famished after sex. I had a glass of wine, and Max made himself a White Russian. I'd started keeping the ingredients there for him.

"Go ahead," I said.

He told me all about Liza Carrow and how he had come to have his picture snapped by the paparazzi the other day.

Yes, they dated a few years ago. No, it wasn't serious. It lasted a short time, and this was before she had landed the role on the soap opera.

I had a heavy, sinking feeling in my stomach as he told me this. Sure, I'd dated before Max and of course he'd dated before me. That was a given. But it was difficult listening to him talk about it now that my feelings for him were becoming so strong. For a few minutes I struggled to wipe my imagination clean of the images of Max fucking her.

Despite the turmoil in my stomach, I drank more wine, and a little more rapidly.

"I didn't love her," he said.

That's the kind of thing someone usually says when they're denying having the same feelings for someone else that they have for you. Was Max telling me something? If he was, I wished he'd just say it.

He continued: "But I won't say I didn't care about her. I still do."

Oh, God…

"But not in the same way that I used to," he went on. "When she called and asked if I would have lunch with her, she told me it was important, and that she really needed to talk to someone she could trust. She said she'd run out of options."

Max took a sip of his White Russian, then reached for another slice of apple.

"She wouldn't tell me over the phone. So I told her I'd meet her for lunch. We weren't there long. We actually only had our drinks and an appetizer. The picture you saw was us leaving after only being in there for maybe twenty minutes or so."

"Why so short?"

Max finished the last sip from his glass. "She told me she doesn't know who the father of the baby is."

"Wow."

"Yeah. Could be any one of four or five guys."

I had a piece of cheese in my mouth but managed to say, "Nice."

Max sighed and looked at me with a grin. His eyebrows rose a little on his forehead. It was the kind of look someone gives you like they're warning you: *Here comes the crazy part.*

"She asked me to say I'm the father."

"Oh, shit."

"But I'm not."

I laughed. "Yeah, I kind of had that figured out already."

Max smiled. "I'm glad you decided to trust me. I told her no, of course." He poured more wine in my glass, and got up to fix himself another drink.

"She really thought you'd do it?"

"She's desperate," Max said.

Liza told him she didn't want to face the media scrutiny of not knowing who the father was. And she said there was no way she was going to start a tabloid frenzy by getting the guys she'd slept with to take paternity tests.

"So," Max said, "I told her it doesn't matter who the father is. If someone asks, she should just say it's private and she's never going to reveal it. That it's something she'll only discuss with her child when the time is right. Oh, and I told her she needed to deny it was me. Not that I'll be in the story for very long. It's really about her. I just got stuck in the wrong place at the wrong time, and someone happened to know we had dated at some point."

"But that was before she was famous, right?"

Max smiled. "You're so smart. That's one of the things I love about you. I know where you were going with that question, and yeah, I think she might have leaked the lie."

"What a bitch."

Max ate.

I sat there thinking not about what we were talking about, so much as what he'd just said: *That's one of the things I love about you.* One of the things? What else was there? And did he love me?

THREE

Sunday morning, lying in bed, we talked in depth about the script. Max wanted to know what I really thought of it.

"I told you, I love it."

"You wouldn't change anything about it?"

I paused, and that was my downfall.

Max said, "Tell me. It's okay. I have a thick skin when it comes to my work."

"Well," I started, then trailed off…

He had been lying on his back, looking up at the ceiling, but he turned toward me and propped his head up in his hand. "Tell me, Olivia."

So I told him.

I loved the characters and I loved what he did with them. But there was one aspect of the girl's reaction at a certain point in the story that I thought would work better if he changed it just a little. It wouldn't throw the storyline off the rails, but it would add another dimension to the girl, making her motives and hopes and dreams more vivid.

Max rolled over and turned away from me. "I can't believe you said that. You think my writing sucks. Way to destroy my confidence."

I moved quickly and grabbed on to his shoulder, turning him back toward me. He had a big smile on his face.

"I'm just kidding," he said.

I smacked his chest. "Jerk."

"So now we're committing domestic violence."

"Yeah," I said, nodding. "And if you fuck with me like that again, it'll be worse." I reached down and grabbed his balls.

He chuckled. "Seriously, though, what you said about the script hadn't even occurred to me."

"Well, you're not a woman. But you did a pretty good job with her, otherwise."

He leaned in to kiss me and when he pulled away I said, "So you see me like you see that character when you wrote her?"

Max nodded. "Weird, huh?"

I didn't say anything.

"I've never believed in fate," he said. "But honestly, when I was writing that—specifically her character—it was different from all the other things I'd ever written before. Or since, actually. I've always had to work on characters for a long time, getting them right, changing things about them. But she was different. She just…came to me…out of nowhere, already perfect."

I looked up at him.

He kissed me again. "Just like you."

Later, as we were getting ready to leave to go out on Max's boat, Krystal came barreling through the front door, looking a little crazed and acting extremely hyper.

She hugged Max, which was odd. Then she started talking rapidly about his movies and how much she loved all of them.

Max was gracious. He either wasn't freaked out by her tornado-like behavior, or he was hiding it really well.

I asked Krystal if she had a cooler.

"Yeah, but it's on the back porch and it's filthy. I'll wash it for you guys!" She was bizarrely excited about the offer.

"We'll just get one at the store," Max said. "Don't go to that trouble."

Krystal looked at me and placed her hand on Max's shoulder. "This guy is amazing, girl!"

I was getting embarrassed for her. She was on something, no doubt. A total trainwreck. Sad.

She asked what we had planned that day, and then said she'd been up all night so she was going to try to get some sleep. I held back from saying that sounded like a great idea, and that maybe she needed to sleep for about a month or so.

When she was gone Max said, "Coke."

"I was thinking something like that."

We were headed out the door when he said, "So, when do I get to see her DVD?"

I knew he was joking so I hit him back with, "Maybe you and I should just make our own."

"Don't tempt me, Olivia."

"Aren't there sharks out here?" I asked Max, as we sat on the stern of his boat, getting ready to swim in the Pacific Ocean. We were a mile or so offshore. The water was calm, but all I could think of was how deep it was and all the creatures below the surface.

"Yep," he said.

"So…why are we doing this again?"

He reached around to my back and untied my bikini top. "It's just one of my ways of getting you naked."

"There are plenty of ways for you to do that without making me shark food."

We were about to skinny-dip. My first time ever.

Max chuckled. "It's going to be fine. Really. California sharks mostly go for blonde girls, anyway."

I watched him toss my bikini top on one of the cushioned seats. "I didn't know you were an expert in marine biology."

"You're feisty today," he said, slipping his fingers under my bikini bottoms. "I like it." He knelt before me and lowered the bottoms. "I like this too." He kissed me once between the legs.

"Excuse me, but why am I the only one who's naked?"

Max remedied the situation by dropping his swim trunks.

I laughed.

Max looked down at himself, then back up at me. "What?"

"Nothing."

He grabbed me. "No, you laughed. What's so funny?"

We were both laughing now. "Your tan lines." I laughed, unable to get more words out.

He picked me up as if he were going to toss me into the ocean. I screamed and held on to him tightly.

"Relax," he said. "I wouldn't do that."

We got into the water and my heart raced. I'd never been in water this deep before, and while I was undeniably nervous about it, having Max there made me feel safe.

"Don't splash," he said. "That's what brings the Great Whites."

Okay, maybe not so safe.

I swam toward him and he took me in his arms. I wrapped mine around his neck. He treaded water for the both of us, holding me up, and I marveled at his strength.

The water lapped at our shoulders and necks. Max gave me a salty kiss, but I didn't care if I swallowed a gallon of the Pacific's water.

Later, out in the bright sunshine of the open sea, Max and I oiled each other up with suntan lotion. All that touching didn't lend itself to a relaxing time lying on towels and soaking up rays.

We ended up fucking on the bow of the boat, our bodies slipping and sliding against each other as Max filled me and thrilled me as though it was our first time.

I talked to Mom and Dad early Sunday evening after getting back home, and they told me they were considering coming out for a visit in two weeks. I wasn't expecting it to be that soon, and I started to mentally prepare for how I would handle the issues of Krystal and Max.

If they saw Krystal in the current shape she was in, it would just give them more ammunition in their war against me being in LA. If they found out about Max, they were likely to kidnap me and haul me off to some institution to have my mind reprogrammed.

Okay, maybe I was being a bit drastic in my worrying. But I really did need to find a way to minimize their interaction with Krystal. As for Max, I would simply tell him I wasn't ready for him to meet my parents, what with our relationship being so new and all, and it would be easy to keep that part of my new life hidden. For now, anyway.

FOUR

Boring week. That is, until Thursday, when I got yet another call from our soon-to-be movie star client, Jacqueline Mathers. Based on all of my previous interactions with her, I thought for sure she was calling to demand another perk. But she wasn't.

"I saw Max Dalton's picture with that woman."

Ah, shit. Not this. She had no idea I was involved with Max, so I had to hide my frustration as she asked me if I believed the denial from Liza Carrow.

"I do," I said.

"I don't. I keep hearing from other actresses that he has a casting couch that's pretty worn out."

She wasn't the first person in town to say that about him. Krystal's friends had been the first at that party a few weeks back. That was when I had my doubts about Max. But no more. I knew who he was, even if no one else did.

"I really don't know," I said. "It's never come up in business meetings with him." There. I tried some mild snark. Maybe she'd drop it.

"As long as I don't have to do that. I mean, I already have the part, so he's not expecting anything, right?"

It was a good thing we were on the phone and I could freely roll my eyes. "Jacqueline, don't worry. It's not going to happen."

It was an odd conversation, to say the least. Not only because of the content itself, but also because I found myself on the verge of defending him like a girlfriend would. I mean, without the cursing and hanging-up on her part.

I kept my cool, changed the subject, and soon we were discussing scheduling and other details of the upcoming shoot.

After our call, I went in to tell Kevin about it. He laughed and said, "She's going to be a handful to deal with."

"Already is."

He was reading something on his iPad and I had a brief flashback of him showing me the screen with that picture of Max and Liza in the tabloid rag.

Kevin said, "Let's close up early and go have a cocktail."

It was just after 4pm. Kevin's suggestion was odd. He'd never asked me to go have a drink with him before, but when the boss wants to shut down and unwind, what can you do?

I figured it might be a good opportunity to pick his brain. I'd been learning a lot in the relatively short time I'd been working for him, but I knew there was so much more to absorb.

We went to an Irish pub around the corner. There was nothing authentically Irish about it beyond the name and the décor. I was beginning to notice that everything in LA was fake: the tans, the hair, the boobs, and even the restaurants. All made for show. No substance. But this was the life I'd chosen and I would learn to fit in.

Kevin ordered a martini, and I had a glass of wine. In the time it took me to nurse my drink to the last drop, Kevin had finished the martini, moved on to a straight Beefeater on the rocks, and was almost done with a second one.

He was getting looser in his story-telling, and I sat in rapt attention listening to the gossip he had inside his head but had never even hinted at. Maybe he was beginning to really trust me as an employee, and maybe this meant I was being formally welcomed as a long-term member of his team.

Oh, what he had in store for the agency! Kevin was extremely ambitious, and when he spoke of where he wanted to see the agency in ten or fifteen years, I believed with every confident word he spoke that he would indeed succeed and see his dreams come to fruition.

I declined a second glass of wine when he asked if I'd like another.

"Come on," he said, "you're with the boss. I won't care if you're a little late tomorrow."

"I really shouldn't."

He lifted his tumbler and threw back the rest of his gin. "You wouldn't turn down a second glass from Max, would you?"

I just looked at him. *Awkard.*

He put his hand on my bare knee, and I suddenly wished like hell that I'd worn pants that day. "Let's get out of here." He squeezed a little and started to slide his hand up my thigh.

"Thanks for the drink," I said, moving off my chair at the bar table. "Are you okay to drive home?"

Kevin stood and moved toward me. "Olivia, I've kept this out of the office but here…I can't help myself."

Ugh. Just what I wanted to hear from my boss. To think just minutes ago I was letting my imagination run wild with a bright future in the business and Kevin as my mentor. So much for that.

"I think you need to call a cab when you leave. Bye, Kevin."

I got out of there quickly and as I got to my car he was jogging toward me. Shit.

"Wait," he said. "I just thought…you know…"

"What?" And then it hit me. "Oh my God. You think because I'm sleeping with Max, I'll sleep with anyone? Just to get noticed and work my way up? Well, you're wrong. And no way will I do it to keep a job. I quit."

"He'll hurt you."

I glared at him. "Maybe so, but at least he has some class."

Kevin stood there shocked. He didn't try to stop me, either with his voice or with physical force. Thank God. I didn't know if I could handle another man being physical with me. I had pepper-spray in my purse, always easily accessible, and Kevin would have ended up lying on the parking lot, writhing around in the gravel, clutching his eyes.

The only eyes with tears in them were mine, though, as I tore out of there and headed for home.

My phone rang three times on the way home. All calls from Kevin. He left a voicemail each time, then sent a text: *I'm sorry. I don't know what got into me. Plz listen to my msgs.*

I didn't listen to them. I called my voicemail and deleted each one before I heard the first syllable out of his mouth. There was nothing he could say to reverse what had happened, and there was no way I was going to work for him anymore. I just couldn't. There'd be no way to get past the weirdness. I had made my decision by the time I pulled up to my apartment complex. I'd told him I was going to quit, and I was going to stand by it.

Even though Kevin's touching had been limited to my knee and my thigh, and it was only for a few seconds, I still felt the need to take a shower. I cried as I scrubbed that leg harder than I'd ever washed it before.

Krystal wasn't home, so I had the place to myself, but I still locked myself in my bedroom. I lay in bed staring up at the ceiling wondering what I would do after quitting the job. Was it pathetic to think that Kevin would give me a recommendation? I was pretty sure I could get one from him. Hell, I was pretty sure I could get anything out of him with the threat of telling Max what had happened. Max could very well cut all business ties with Kevin and his agency, but that would mean hurting Jacqueline as well. She was innocent in all of this and considering she was under contract with Kevin, it wasn't as though she could go off on her own and keep the role in Max's film.

Damnit. My mind was swirling with confusion and too many side issues that I didn't need to worry about at the time. What I needed to be thinking about was how to handle being unemployed, surviving in LA, telling my parents all of this or lying to them when they came to visit, and how to explain to Max why I was no longer working for Kevin.

Of course, I could fake forgiveness and go back to work there and make everything seem fine. Except I'd only be making it seem fine to everyone else. It wouldn't be fine with me at all. And I was finished with the part of my life where my happiness, comfort and well-being took a backseat to anyone.

FIVE

I didn't even bother contacting Kevin on Friday morning. No phone call, no text, no email, nothing. I just didn't show up. I didn't hear from him, either, which pretty much told me he knew I'd never be back.

I spent the day trying to figure out what I would do next in terms of work. No good ideas immediately came to mind, and I decided to put off the worrying for the weekend. Bright and early Monday morning, my new job would be finding a new job.

Max texted me around noon: *House or boat this weekend?*

Just reading it gave me a smile, even though I hadn't yet told him about not working for Kevin anymore, and for all Max knew I was at the office.

Me: *What? We can't do both?;)*

Max: *We can do whatever you want.*

Me: *Okay, how about you dress up as a pirate and rescue me from danger and have your way with me on your boat?*

Max: *As long as I don't have to talk in a pirate voice.*

Me: *Oh, then forget it. :(*

We decided we would play it by ear—no firm plans, just do whatever we wanted hour by hour. It sounded like heaven to me.

But I knew I'd have to mention the whole Kevin thing to him. I just couldn't decide whether to do it at the start of our weekend. I wanted to hold back until Sunday so our weekend wouldn't be tainted by the unpleasantness of the story, but I also thought Max might want to know right away. I decided I would play that by ear also—if the time seemed right, I'd bring it up.

Krystal came home around 11 a.m. I was sitting in the den, reading some of the Hollywood tabloids on my iPad and having a cup of coffee.

"Are you sick?" she asked as she came through the door.

"No. Worse."

"What's wrong?"

She sat down beside me and I told her the whole sordid story. Tears began to flow again. Krystal hugged me and I sobbed into her shoulder.

She handed me a tissue. "What did Max say?"

"I haven't told him yet."

"He's gonna be pissed."

I nodded as I wiped my eyes.

"At least you're not in my situation," she said.

I looked at her. "What do you mean?"

"Come on, Olivia. You know."

I looked down at my hands that were balling the tissue anxiously.

She said, "You saw the DVD. You saw me come in the other day after staying up all night on coke."

"Jesus, Krystal. Cocaine?"

She nodded and shrugged, and told me everything. It was a confession of sorts, almost like I was a priest and she was a parishioner. I listened with sympathy, and at one point I grabbed her hand as she started to cry.

"I got mixed up in this because of the money," she explained. "Now…I can't get out. I don't know what to do."

"Why can't you just stop?"

"And do what?" Her voice came out with more than a little touch of frustration, but I knew it wasn't directed at me. "I'll never get a real acting job. I'm fucked."

"No, you're not."

"I really am," she said, taking a deep breath and letting it out forcefully through pursed lips. "I'm in debt. Big time."

It was the drugs. She was getting paid to do porn, but a big chunk of it had been going to feed her coke habit. Then she started getting it on "credit" with the dealer, and now, to my horror, she was sitting there telling me she owed the guy about twenty thousand.

It turns out the dealer was also the guy hooking her up with various porn gigs. It was almost like he was a pimp, I thought. And then, just as that thought entered my mind, she said that's what the guy had in mind for payback. He was going to pimp her out.

"Holy shit" was the only reaction that came to mind. What the hell had she gotten herself into? "It isn't Marco, is it?" I had met that guy weeks ago when I walked in on the two of them just as they were probably getting ready to have sex in the den. It didn't take me long to pick up on his creepiness.

"No, not him," she said. "He's got his own problems. I haven't even talked to him in like a week or so."

"Can you just…leave? I mean, go back to Ohio? Get away from here?"

She shook her head. "And, what? Go back to my parents' house? Ha. Very funny."

"I didn't mean that, I just—"

"I know," she said, "I'm sorry."

We sat there for a little while longer, commiserating with each other. Here we were, two Midwestern girls trying to make it in the big city, both now totally screwed by failure.

Later, around 5:30, Max came to get me.

Krystal was in her room taking a nap. She'd been in there for almost two hours. I told Max before we left I needed to check on her. I cracked the door just a little, saw that she was facing away from the door. She was sleeping, breathing deeply, and was probably getting the only rest and relaxation she'd had in a while. I decided to leave her a note on the kitchen counter.

"Coming down off a high?" Max said.

I looked up from the paper. "You have no idea."

"What is it?"

I folded up the paper and laid the pen on top of it. "I'll tell you later."

We got to Max's house and the first thing he did was run a warm bath. We lathered each other up. I faced him as he massaged the shampoo into my scalp, and I massaged his cock.

It started when he told me to tilt my head back so he could rinse my hair. "Hold on so you don't fall."

Instead of reaching for his shoulders or his waist, I took his semi-hard erection into my hand.

He laughed. "That should work."

"Gee, I wonder if that's what you wanted me to do all along."

"No."

My mouth dropped open. "What? Fine, then."

"If I wanted you to do that, I would just tell you to."

"Oh really."

He looked at me. "Touch it, Olivia."

The warm water sluiced through my hair and ran down my back in soapy waves, and Max got fully hard in my hand. I loved how it got longer and thicker under my touch. When I looked down I saw now that he had grown to a length that broke the surface, with at least half of him straight up out of the water.

"Like a periscope," I joked.

He closed his eyes and shook his head. "Maybe you should do stand up comedy."

"You think?"

"No."

I squeezed him—hard.

"Easy now."

Max pulled me against him and I slipped my hand away. His erection was pressed against my stomach—slipping and sliding around on it—making me want it inside me.

He pressed his lips to mine, pulling my tongue into his mouth, then sucking on it like I sucked when his cock was in my mouth.

Max kissed his way down my neck, then across the top of my chest. He pulled me closer, up onto his lap. His erection was perfectly notched in my cleft and I just wanted him to do it, do it, do it…

But he didn't. He teased me, rocking his hips as he moved me back and forth so I was sliding along the length of his cock. Which, honestly, was almost enough to make me come by itself. But I didn't want that. I wanted to come with him inside me.

I pressed my face to the top of his wet head as he sucked on my nipples.

"I hate not being inside you, Olivia."

"Then do it."

"Not just now," he said. "Always. I wish I could be inside you all day, every day."

And with those words, he shifted a certain way and entered me. I moved my hips to ease him in. Each time we did this, I loved the way he stretched my tightness.

This was slow, sensual sex. It was more like making love than fucking. I wondered if he felt that way, too, but I didn't dare ask him. I feared not getting the response I wanted to hear.

And as I thought about that—while sliding up and down on him—my eyes started to tear up a little.

When Max noticed he said, "Are you okay?"

"Yes. Everything is…perfect."

Max pulled me closer and we kissed as we climaxed together.

After the shower, I put on one of his button-down shirts and Max wore only a pair of jeans as we sat at a bar table in his kitchen and ate dinner.

"Something's on your mind," he said. "Is it Krystal?"

Actually, that wasn't it at all. I was distracted by the ongoing debate in my head about whether to tell him what happened with Kevin and the fallout from it. I also was on the verge of asking him if he had felt the same thing I did in the bathtub. But the Krystal issue was good enough for now. Plus, I'd already promised him I'd tell him.

And so I did—complete with all the details she had given me.

"Jesus," he said. "Twenty grand. Where's she going to get that?"

"No idea."

"You know what that means." Max stood and took our empty plates to the sink. "She's going to end up working it off."

I got up and walked toward him. "I can't decide which is worse. That or the coke."

"Both."

I stood next to him as he rinsed off the dishes and put them in the dishwasher. His face was a mask of concern, and I assumed it was about Krystal, even though he hardly knew her.

"What are you thinking?" I asked.

He closed the dishwasher, started it, and picked up a towel to dry his hands. "Let's get her out of trouble."

"What do you mean?"

"I'll pay the guy off."

Whoa.

"On one condition, though," he said. "She has to check into rehab."

"Are you serious? You'd do that?"

"Yes."

"But you don't even know her."

Max took me in his arms. "But you do. I'm not going to let you stand by helplessly watching a friend ruin her life."

"Max…I don't think—"

"Let me do this. Let *us* do this."

SIX

I woke up Saturday morning, lying on my side. I had my back to Max, and he was just about ready to slide inside me. I looked over my shoulder at him. He was looking down, watching what he was doing. "I could wake up like this every day. Awesome alarm clock."

"Funny. But I can't help it, Olivia."

"I was being serious," I said, and put my head back down while Max brought us both to an early morning orgasm.

After we showered Max drove us to Marina Del Rey, where we boarded his boat and set off for Catalina Island. I had heard of the place and was under the impression that it was only for the wildly rich and the tourists. I guess I qualified as a tourist, and since I was with Max, the rich part took care of itself.

Max pulled the boat up to the marina. A dockhand was there and called out to him. "Hello, Mr. Dalton." The guy climbed aboard and said he would take care of the docking. I saw Max slip him a hundred dollar bill before we got off the boat. Valet parking at a marina. Who knew?

We spent a good part of the late morning and early afternoon taking a tour of the island. It was gorgeous—lush green trees and bushes, incredible views of the ocean and the island's various canyons—like nothing I'd ever experienced.

And it only got more intriguing, as the tour guide signaled for us to look in various directions throughout the ride, to see the incredible wildlife the island had to offer. We saw wild turkeys and pigs, two bald eagles, and even buffalo.

"I love this place," Max said.

I was holding on to his arm as we sat in the jeep. I held on tighter when I saw the almost boyish way he marveled at the outdoors.

"It's beautiful," I said, resting my head on his shoulder.

"Makes you not want to go back to the city, doesn't it?"

I looked up at his face and saw that he was deadly serious. The truth was, I didn't care where we were. I just wanted to be with him. *Needed* to be with him.

Later in the afternoon, we took our shoes off and sat on a little beach area. Off in the distance, sea lions occupied the rock jetties. We were told they could be aggressive, and to keep an eye on them. They were far enough away not to pose a threat, and we didn't have any food with us anyway.

I was starting to feel guilty about keeping the Kevin story from Max. He deserved to know. He was going to find out one way or another. The idea of keeping it from him so it wouldn't ruin our weekend hadn't been a good idea at all. While it spared him from thinking about it, delaying did nothing for me. Despite all the enjoyment of the afternoon, thoughts of telling Max what happened lingered close by, threatening to spoil the day.

So it was on that peaceful little spot of land that I said, "I have something to tell you…."

I told him everything, ending with an apology for not telling him sooner.

"I don't care about that," he said, holding me tight. "What a fuckwit."

"A what?"

Max gave a little chuckle. “Fuckwit. Like an idiot, but much worse. One of my favorite words.”

“I’ve never heard you use it.”

“I save it for special occasions, and this is definitely one of them. The deal with Jacqueline Mathers is the biggest thing that’s ever happened to him. I guess he didn’t think about that.”

“Are you going to drop her?”

Max shook his head. “No, she’s good. Perfect for the role. I’m not going to start from scratch just because Kevin makes stupid decisions about who to try to fuck.”

This was going easier than I thought. I had actually expected him to be angry—maybe somewhat at me for not telling him, and certainly at Kevin for doing what he did. “You don’t sound mad at him.”

“I’m not,” he said, without hesitating. “He’s pathetic. And I don’t think for a minute you would give in to him.”

Now that we’d settled that part of it, I felt free to express how worried I was for myself. “I hate that he did it, mostly because I have to start over now, you know?”

We had shifted so that Max was sitting behind me, and held my back close to his chest. He kissed me on the top of my head, and kept his lips there as we sat in silence for a moment. Finally, he broke it.

"Work with me."

I had been relaxing so much that my eyes were almost closed. They flew open when I heard his words.

"What?"

"You heard me."

"Yeah, but…" My voice trailed off. I was stunned by his suggestion.

He kissed me on my head again and said, "I've been thinking about what I'm going to do when I stop producing. You know I just want to write. That's what I'm going to do. But I'll need an assistant, someone who will read all my stuff and not bullshit me with empty praise. Just like you did the other day. You were brilliant, Olivia. Your ideas made the story so much better."

I moved so I could face him. "You're serious."

He nodded and reached up to touch my cheek. "Don't worry about anything. And I know you by now—you're thinking I'm doing this just to help you out. I'm not. You impressed me from that first meeting. I'd hire you even if you weren't sleeping with me."

My smile must have stretched across my entire face, and Max returned one just as big, then said, “Of course, we’ll have to be careful how we proceed.”

“What do you mean?”

“I’ll pay you as an independent contractor, not as a direct employee.”

“Why’s that?”

“Because then you can’t turn around and sue me for sexually harassing you on the job every day.”

I laughed and leaned forward to kiss him. “Every day? You promise?”

“Try to stop me.”

On the boat ride home, I told him my parents would be coming for a visit. “And I’m worried.”

“About what?”

Max was driving the boat and I was sitting on his lap. I put on one of his baseball caps and put my hair through the hole in the back, a makeshift ponytail to keep it from whipping him in the face.

"My living situation, for one thing," I said. "They're going to wonder about Krystal. Remember, she was my sister's friend growing up?"

"Right. Well, maybe she won't be around if she takes us up on the offer to help and checks into rehab. Then you can just say she's out of town or something."

"True." He had a point. It was a justifiable lie. I'd be protecting Krystal's confidentiality. My stomach churned with nervousness as I considered how to tell him I wasn't sure about having him meet my parents.

We hadn't been together very long, but several times during our time together, it seemed as though Max knew exactly what I was thinking. I knew he wasn't literally reading my mind, but it was still odd at times.

Just as it was when, without me having said one word about it, Max said, "You're worried about telling them about me." He said it flatly, as though he didn't like the idea at all.

"My family can be complicated. It's not that I don't want you to meet them. Just not right now."

Max slowed the boat down as we approached Marina Del Rey. "It's up to you. I'll just miss you while they're here."

SEVEN

Krystal was vegging out in front of the TV when I got home Sunday afternoon. She looked like she'd gotten some sleep, and actually smiled when I walked in the door.

She muted the TV. "Good weekend?"

"Yeah, pretty great. How about you?"

"Oh, so good," she said, letting out a huge sigh. "I slept most of yesterday. Turned my phone off and turned the world off. It was heaven. Actually, it's still off." Her previously happy expression turned to frowning worry. "I keep dreading turning it on and seeing the missed calls and texts."

I guessed that now was as good a time as ever to tell her what Max had offered, so I did, with no beating around the bush. I just said, "Max wants to pay the twenty grand and get you out of trouble."

She stared at me. "You told him?"

I nodded, then shifted uncomfortably in the chair, waiting for her to recoil as Max predicted she would do at first.

And she did.

Krystal threw her head back on the pillow. "I can't do that. I'll never be able to pay him back."

"You don't have to. He said—"

She sat to an upright position. "The hell I don't. I'm not a charity case."

I slowly shook my head. "You're right, you're not. But think about this. It's an easy way out."

"And then what? I'll be right back in it up to my fucking eyes before I know it."

This is the part that would be the hardest, I thought. Offering that kind of money to someone was a potential blow to their pride, but the rehab part of the deal could be a lot worse.

I moved next to her on the couch and put my arm around her. "No, you won't. Hear me out, okay?"

I explained it to her, and she took it surprisingly well. By the time we were done, she had promised me that she'd think about it.

"One thing, though," I said. "Let me know soon, okay? And in the meantime..."

"I know, stay away from that crowd."

Jesus. I felt like her mother, but I knew it was the right thing to do. She needed help and Max's offer was a once-in-a-lifetime chance to get her life back on track. She'd take the deal. I just had to give her a little time.

"Oh, hey," she said as I was getting up from the couch. "What did Max say about the Kevin thing and you leaving your job?"

I didn't want to tell her that Max had offered me a job as his assistant. It might have only made her feel worse about what lay ahead for her. While she was facing rehab and getting her entire life back on track, my problem had seemed to work itself out in a matter of days.

So I just said, "He called Kevin a 'fuckwit'."

"A what?"

"That's what I said."

We enjoyed a good laugh over the word and it saved me from having to tell her the rest of the story.

Later that evening, I talked to my parents and found out they'd be arriving that Friday. Grace was coming, along with her kids, but my brother-in-law was staying home.

I felt a mixture of happiness and dread about the whole thing. Maybe it would go well. Or maybe it would just go fast. After all, they'd only be here for a couple of days.

I had to warn Krystal about it. She had known my family for years and I didn't want them to see her in the state she was currently in. Part of that was for her own good—she'd be totally uncomfortable, especially around Grace. Part of it was for mine—if my parents found out I lived with someone who was into cocaine and did porn, I'd never be able to deal with their fury.

"They're not going to stay here, are they?" she asked.

"No. God, no. They'll stay at a hotel. But I know they'll want to see where I live."

"Okay, well, I can hide in my bedroom or something. Keep the door closed. You can tell them I'm working or something. They won't want to see my room."

Maybe she'd forgotten how nosey my parents were. "We'll work it out." I started to head back to my room. "Oh, and one other thing. I'm not telling them about Max. And they don't know about me quitting the agency. So, if for some reason you do end up seeing them....you know, just go along with whatever I say."

She laughed. "Damn, girl. You're having to hide everything."

"Story of my life."

EIGHT

Max called me first thing Monday morning and told me he'd talked to the editor of the tabloid.

The editor had already heard from Liza Carrow, and said they were going to run a story clearing up their previous one.

"That sounds easy enough," I said, "but didn't you want to give him a bunch of shit for what they did?"

"I wanted to. Definitely. But it's better this way. If I had come across like an ass to the guy, he might never take my calls again in the future when their next bullshit story runs. Which I don't think it will, but you never know."

I was silent for a moment.

"Of course," he said, "next time I'd probably go over there and bust the place up with a baseball bat."

"Then you'd end up on the *front* page."

"Excellent point, once again," he said. "What would I do without you?"

Late that afternoon, I got a call from Kevin. Of course I let it go to voicemail. When my phone chirped, I checked the message. I hated hearing his voice, but I listened anyway. Big mistake. I should have deleted it without giving it a single second's worth of my attention.

"Olivia, I won't bother you anymore after this. But let's please discuss what happened. I'm really sorry. I need you. I mean, I need you *here*. Working." Pause. "Think about it. Please?"

Pathetic. He was begging, and there was only one reason: he was afraid he would lose out on the Jacqueline Mathers deal.

I was feeling particularly spiteful that day, so I decided I would let myself feel no guilt for letting him wonder and worry.

On Thursday night, I told Max that Krystal said she wanted to take him up on the offer. We were at his house, spending time together before my parents would arrive the next day.

I was brushing my teeth in the master bath when Max put his arms around me from behind. "I'm going to miss you."

"It's only a few days," I said, with my mouth full of toothpaste. Real sexy.

"So you're not going to miss me?"

I rinsed out my mouth, and when I bent over Max lifted my shirt. I was wearing one of his t-shirts, and nothing else, ready for bed. He cupped my ass and gave it a squeeze.

With my mouth now free of toothpaste, I wiped my face with a towel. "Of course I'll miss you."

"A few days of not being inside you is going to kill me."

I stood straight up, still facing the mirror, and saw that familiar intensity on Max's face. He reached around to my front and took my breasts in his hands and caressed them beneath the t-shirt. My nipples puckered at his touch, and I pushed back to feel his erection. He was wearing only boxers and so far, they were still holding his cock back, although I thought I could feel the head as Max pressed against me.

He separated my legs and told me to stand on my tip-toes.

"I want to see your face in the mirror when I go inside you."

We watched each other's reactions as his cock pushed into me. Max kissed my neck as we kept our eyes trained on each other. We stood like that for a minute or so, just feeling each other—him feeling my tight warmth, me feeling his rigid length and thickness.

He turned me around and lifted me off the floor, kissing me, devouring my mouth. He carried me out of the bathroom and over to his bed, laying me down on my back. I wrapped my legs around his waist, urging him to push inside me.

I needed him. Needed him to make love to me....

I reached down between us and gripped the firm length of his cock. Smoothing my hands over the shaft, and then back up to the tip, I felt a droplet of liquid there. He was ready to go.

Max suddenly stood, pulling me to a sitting position on the edge of the bed. Wordlessly, he removed his boxers, guided his cock toward my mouth, and I opened for him.

I tasted his precome as my mouth covered the plump crown.

"Damn, Olivia. You're amazing."

His words encouraged me. I looked up at him and met his gaze. Wow, that stare. That animalistic stare, laced with intense need. A look that I never, ever wanted to get used to. And to think I brought this out in him.

My mouth was filled with his thickness. My hand held him at the base as I took as much as I could of him between my lips, across my tongue. My other hand reached for his balls. I cupped them, this time more firmly than I had in the past, just as I'd seen him to do himself when he masturbated for me on the plane.

"God, Olivia, I love that...."

I kept my eyes trained up, watching the facial expressions created by what I was doing to him. I smiled around his cock.

"Take it deep," he said, with a soft edge of command in his tone.

I worked my lips down the shaft as far as it would go and felt the head at the back of my throat. I couldn't keep it there for very long, so I slid my mouth up the length. He was wet, so wet, ready to come....

He felt like he was getting bigger with each throb, and I thought he was about to flood my mouth. If he had, it would have been fine with me. But Max didn't want to, just yet.

He pulled back and his cock left my mouth with a little wet *pop* and *smack* sound.

"Not yet, Liv."

Liv. No one had ever called me that before. The sound of that word—the nickname Max had just created for me—sent a tingle through my nerves. He'd given me a name. One that he and he alone had used or would ever use.

Hearing "Liv" made me think of "love" and "live." Thoughts of how I knew I loved him and was living for him flooded my mind and my heart, but I managed to keep from blurting it out.

I just wanted him inside me. Badly.

"I don't want to come yet," he said. "I want this to last, we're going to come together."

Max gently moved me back on the bed and pulled the t-shirt over my head. Then he dropped to his knees on the floor. His mouth dove for my pussy and his tongue was vigorously fluttering my folds. Then I felt his mouth seal around my clit as he sucked the tight little bud between his lips.

"Tell me what you want, Liv."

God, there it was again. That name.

"I want to come with you deep inside me." I managed to get the words out through my uneven breaths.

He kept his mouth where it was. Teasing. Torturing. And I knew he wanted me to beg.

"Do it, Max. I need you in me."

He moved swiftly on top of me, and was effortlessly inside me in the flash of a second. His rigid length stroked along my slick flesh. He pushed deeper and I arched my back in response.

"Yes!" The word just flew out of me.

"Fuck, Liv, you're so perfect. So tight. So warm. I want to be here forever."

"M-me…too….don't stop…ever…."

Max got into a long, even, hard rhythm, moving in and out of me—almost all the way to the tip of his cock, then back in to the hilt.

"Are you mine?" he breathed into my ear.

"Yours. Yes, I'm yours."

Max sat up between my legs. He remained inside me as he grabbed the t-shirt that was lying next to my head. Many times before, while we had sex, he would hold my arms above my head with just one of his large hands wrapped around my wrists. This time he was going to do it differently.

"Do you trust me, Olivia?"

A spark of adrenaline flashed in my chest and I started moving my hips in little gyrating motions, massaging his cock with my pussy.

"Yes."

Max wrapped the t-shirt around my wrists, then tied the ends through the iron posts of the headboard. I was restrained now, and he was totally free.

He reached for one of the extra pillows and held it as he turned me over onto my stomach. The t-shirt tightened as I rolled and it twisted a little, but there was no pain from it.

Max lifted my hips with his hand and slid the pillow beneath me. It raised my ass up, giving him better access to me. He spread my legs, making me even more open and vulnerable. All his....

I felt his hot breath on my neck as he lowered again, his arms on either side of me holding him up, his cock rubbing against my ass.

Oh, God...was this it? My first anal? I wasn't sure I was ready for it. I'd never wanted it before, but now, with Max, I wanted everything.

"Don't worry," he said, "I'm not going to do that."

Jesus, what was it with him always practically reading my mind? Or was I just that easy to read?

"It's okay," I said.

"No, we'll have to work up to it. And I can't wait right now."

The head of his cock pushed between my wet folds again, and Max was sliding into me in one long stroke.

"I want you, Liv. And I'm going to have all of you, every way, eventually."

"Yes, yes..."

I thought he would just do it. I was in position, and while I probably really wasn't ready physically, my mind was already in a place that would give up anything for Max. Anything to please him, to fulfill all of his needs as he did mine.

I felt his thumb press against me and then ever so slowly he worked it into my ass.

My head dropped and my face was buried in the pillow. Like he'd done other times we were having sex, Max pulled the pillow away and said, "I want to hear you."

I was breathing heavily and he was causing little whimpers to escape from my mouth, as he worked his thumb in farther.

The pressure was intense, a great feeling of being filled. His cock stroked along my inner walls and having his thumb there maximized the sensation.

I was hopeless to hold off. I just couldn't stop myself. I felt the spasms in my abdomen. They came quickly and fiercely, and so did I.

And I felt the warm slickness of Max's semen pumping into me.

"God, Liv...you drive me crazy in every way..."

NINE

My parents arrived the next afternoon with Grace and the baby, my newest niece. The older one stayed at home with my brother-in-law because she had come down with a cold at the last minute. Grace almost didn't come because of that, but felt okay about it when her mother-in-law came to stay at their house for a few days.

They drove from Ohio so they were all tired by the time they got to their hotel. It was only ten minutes from my apartment and I headed over there when Grace called to say Dad was getting them checked into the rooms.

We sat around for a while and the focus was mostly on the baby, of course. I couldn't believe how different she looked after having not seen her for just a few months.

Dad was sitting in a chair and nodding off, but snapped awake when the subject of food came up.

We decided to keep it simple and cheap, and just went to a chain restaurant.

"People drive like crazy around here," Dad said.

Mom agreed and said it was probably the drugs.

"They have drugs in Ohio, you know," I said.

Dad shot me a look like I was still a kid and should be quiet instead of pointing out a simple fact that didn't fall in line with my parents' predetermined opinion.

"We're only here for a few days," Grace said. "Can we not argue?" Ever the diplomat, but I knew she agreed with them. She'd followed their path in life and thought like they did, but we still had that sisterly bond that no one could break and if she had any plans to give me grief about leaving Ohio, she'd wait until we were alone.

After dinner we drove around LA for a little while. Grace wanted to see more of the city, and I think my mom did as well, though she reluctantly took Grace's side when my dad said it was dark and we wouldn't be able to see anything.

"Dad, this whole city is lights," Grace said.

Dad came up with another reason not to ride around. "Well, it's getting kind of late."

"It's 7:40," Mom said. "With the time difference, it's not even five o'clock to us."

Dad sighed. "All right, but we're keeping the windows up and the doors locked."

Grace and I looked at each other in the backseat and rolled our eyes.

Later, back at the hotel, we were all in my parents' room. Grace and the baby were staying in an adjacent room, and the two were linked by a door.

This is when Dad started his pitch in earnest, telling me I should really think about coming home, there was plenty to do there in the way of work, that's where my friends were, etc. And, just for added guilt, he said, "What would you do if something happened to one of us?"

"What do you mean?"

Dad shrugged. "An accident. One of us gets sick. Anything. You're so far away."

"It doesn't take long by plane," I said.

"That's not cheap."

He was right, of course. It wasn't cheap to get a ticket for a flight from LA to Ohio on short notice. What he didn't know, and what I couldn't tell them, was that I wouldn't have to buy a ticket. Max would fly me home in a heartbeat.

He dropped the issue, probably just thinking of his next line of attack. Mom had stayed silent while Dad and I discussed the distance issue, but then she picked up when he stopped.

"You haven't been back to Las Vegas, I hope?"

"I go there every weekend."

Mom looked at me in shock. Dad cut his eyes at me.

"I'm kidding," I said.

Grace handed me the baby, who looked at me and smiled. I smiled back, thinking how nice it was to have at least one relative who wasn't judging me.

"They're just worried about you," Grace said a little later.

"I know, but it gets old."

"I'm worried about you, too, you know. Especially after that whole thing with Chris."

"He's gone," I said. "And I doubt he'll be back."

We were in the adjacent hotel room. Mom and Dad had gone to bed, the baby was asleep, and it was getting close to 11:00.

"I know you are, but seriously, Grace, wouldn't you rather be here? I mean, you saw the city. There's never a boring minute here."

"Maybe I like boring."

That couldn't be more true. And it couldn't have made me more sad for her. Yes, I was being judgmental, but I'd been on the receiving end of judgment myself for too long.

Grace said, "So, what's up with Krystal?"

Jesus. What a topic. One that I didn't want to talk about. One that would only confirm that she and my parents were right about this probably being a bad scene for me. One that would give them the wrong impression about how wonderful things were really going when you considered everything with Max.

I said, "I hardly ever see her. She's always working at that restaurant or going to casting calls." There. I lied. But I had to. And it worked. She moved on to something else.

"What do you do when you're not working?" she asked.

I could have answered truthfully with the one-liner that popped into my head: *When I'm not working, I do Max.* But that was a little joke I had to keep to myself.

I gave her a generic response—hanging out with friends, still trying to see all of the city and the surrounds, going to the gym....

"Have you met any boys yet?"

Boys.

I must have hesitated just slightly too long because I clearly gave away the answer.

We were lying on the bed. I was on my back, she was on her stomach, and when she sensed I had something juicy to tell, she flipped over on her side to face me.

"Ohhh, you have. Do tell."

So I told. Even about the trip to Napa. But not about New York.

"And…remember when I told you that someone saved me from Chris that night at my apartment door?"

"Yeah. A neighbor, but…it was this guy?"

I nodded.

"Wow."

"I know. And I'm sorry I lied to you about him."

"Don't worry about it. So, what movies has he done?"

I told her, and she recognized a couple of them. She liked one of them so much, she had a DVD of it at home.

She was silent for a moment. Then another, "Wow," but this time softer, like she was trying to imagine what it would be like to live her younger sister's life. "You look happy, but…you kind of also don't."

Shit. She could read me well.

"It's just that I'm pretty sure he's serious about me, but I'm afraid that I feel more than he does. You know?"

"Have you brought it up with him?"

"Oh, God no."

"Why not?"

I took a deep breath and exhaled slowly. When I thought about this, my chest got tight and my stomach churned.

"I don't want to push things too fast," I said.

She nodded. "So, have you slept with him?"

"Yes." I closed my eyes.

"Then it's serious."

Sometimes Grace could be really rational and insightful. Sometimes she could be really naïve. And sometimes she could be both of those things at almost the same time.

"I don't know," I said.

"What does he look like?"

I got my phone out of my bag to do a Google Image search. I'd had it on mute all night, and when I swiped the screen I saw that I had missed a text from Max.

It read: *I'm coming to get you.*

"Hang on," I said to Olivia. "Have to text somebody back."

"Him?"

"Yeah."

I texted: *What!?*

Max: *That was a joke and it was two hours ago.*

Me: *You couldn't find me anyway.*

Max: *You underestimate me.*

Me: *I know. It's a bad habit.*

Max: *Please keep doing it. Makes it easier to impress you.*

Me: *So you weren't really coming to get me?*

Max: *No. My dreams will have to suffice tonight.*

Me: *Awwww.*

Max: *Did you just see a puppy?*

Me: *What?*

Max: *'Awwww'? People say that when they see a puppy or a baby. I was hoping you would say 'I'll make it up to you'.*

Me: *I'll make it up to you.*

Max: *Awwww.*

Me: *Haha! I have to get back to talking to my sister. By the smile on my face she might assume the worst.*

Max: *She'd be smart to. Talk to you tomorrow. Miss you.*

Me: *Me too.*

I closed the texts and pulled up the browser, went to Google Images and found a picture of Max.

"Here. This is him."

I handed her my phone.

She looked at the picture, then looked at me, then back at the picture. "Get out of here. You're seeing this hottie?"

I raised my eyebrows. "Gee, thanks."

"No, no. I didn't mean it like that." She burst out laughing. "That came out wrong. It's just…wow, he's gorgeous."

"And nice, and funny, and kind-hearted, generous, interesting, exciting, creative—"

She interrupted: "Honest?"

"Yeah. Well, except for this one thing." I told her about Liza Carrow.

"I see why he didn't tell you right away, though."

"I know. I wasn't fair to him when it happened. But we're past that."

She handed the phone back to me. "Hate to say this, but I'm jealous."

"Oh, stop."

"He's no Brian. Speaking of which, I need to call and see how things are going there."

While she made her call, I looked at Max's picture, then at the texts we'd just exchanged. Damnit, I had fallen hard for him, and I was so in love there was no turning back.

I went into the bathroom to wash my face and brush my teeth while she finished up her call. I was starting to get tired and couldn't wait to get to sleep. With all the talk of Max, though, combined with a little talk of Chris, and the random way my fears reared their ugly head, I hoped I wouldn't have one of those nightmares again while I slept in the same room with my sister.

TEN

The next morning, we all ate at a nice restaurant that served a great breakfast. My dad said it was too expensive a place to eat, and when I said I was buying, we spent the next ten minutes with him and my mom arguing that I "can't" and then "shouldn't have to" pay for all of us to eat when we could grab something quick at a fast-food place.

I won the debate, mostly because I just started walking into the place and Grace followed.

After breakfast my parents wanted to see where I worked. *Gulp*. I hadn't even thought about that. Later the night before, after Grace got off the phone with her husband, I told her the rest of what was going on with me: quitting the job, but soon working with Max. She promised not to say anything to my parents. Luckily, it was a Saturday, so all we had to do was drive by the building and I pointed while saying, "That's it. Just a regular building."

Whew.

We spent the better part of the afternoon taking a tour of Universal Studios. It was something I hadn't done yet since coming to LA, so I didn't mind doing something so "touristy."

I got to push the stroller around for a while and at one point when my parents and Grace went to use the restrooms, I sat on a bench in the shade, alone with my baby niece. People—mostly women and girls—stopped by and cooed at her, telling me how beautiful she was. I just thanked them, not telling them she wasn't mine.

I'd never even thought about being a mother before. Certainly not like my own mother had, and not even like Grace had. But that was the first time I'd experienced anything resembling the desire to have a child. Definitely a strange feeling for me.

I got a text from Max: *Let me treat your family to dinner.*

Me: *Well, hello to you to.*

Max: *Hey there, dream girl.*

I smiled at that, but it didn't last long. He wanted to take my family out for dinner?

Me: *We talked about this. Not ready.*

Max: *I don't have to be there. Let me make reservations at a nice place. You take them.*

Me: *Where is this coming from?*

Max: *I just want to do something nice for you. And for them.*

I sighed and thought about what I'd write back. It was a very generous offer, and I wasn't surprised by it, considering that's just how Max was. But I really did think he was trying to angle his way into meeting them.

Me: *Why do you want to meet them so bad?*

Max: *Because they're your family. But I don't have to. Just let me set this up.*

Me: *Are you sure?*

Max: *Yes, but you have to promise me one thing.*

Me: *Oh God. Does it involve handcuffs?*

Max: *I hadn't thought of that, but we can try.*

Me: *Ha! Seriously. What is it?*

Max: *You'll come with me to meet my mom.*

Shit. He was really pushing this. How often does a guy insist on meeting your family and you meeting his? He was clearly serious about us. It showed in his actions, but for some reason, not his words. Several times I had to hold myself back from blurting out the fact that I was in love with him but had thankfully spared myself the potential embarrassment and, worse, abandonment. I was sure it would be too much for him, too soon.

But all this family meeting stuff… Maybe I just needed to let him go at his own pace. He had walls. High walls. Maybe even higher than mine. But those walls were coming down, and for the first time in a while I was giving him a peek over my barrier. He was letting me over his, too. Maybe I'd let him take the lead on the timing of all this.

I texted: *We'll talk about it, but yes I'll meet her.*

Max: *Let me work on dinner and I'll get back to you.*

Me: *OK. Thank you. That's so nice.*

Max got us a reservation at Spago in Beverly Hills, a restaurant owned by the famed chef Wolfgang Puck.

Carrying out Max's offer to treat us to dinner was like something out of an espionage movie.

We texted back and forth about how to handle the bill. If the waiter said everything was taken care of, that would raise a major investigation by my parents. So Max had arranged for the manager to inform the waiter to take my card as if I were paying, but they would just put it on Max's running tab.

"We still haven't seen your apartment," Mom said at one point.

I had a mouthful of our appetizer and stopped chewing, but quickly brought my napkin up to my mouth and held up one finger. I knew they'd want to see it—why wouldn't they—but somehow had fooled myself into thinking they wouldn't remember. Right. Like parents wouldn't want to see where you're living. Especially mine. As I finished swallowing, I actually found myself surprised that it had taken them this long to begin with.

"Maybe when we leave here," I said. "I need to get home anyway. I don't have another day's worth of clothes and I might as well just stay there tonight."

I looked at Grace, who had an expression on her face like she knew something. Maybe she suspected I had a date with Max or something. If so, she was wrong.

"The prices here are outrageous," Dad said, a little too loud.

"Dad, don't worry about it. I told you, I've got this."

He shook his head, and looked down at the menu again. Thank God he didn't restart the debate we'd had in the car earlier. My parents insisted that they pay for dinner, and I said it was my treat, and it was on from there. I finally got the upper hand by explaining to them that I was on my own now, with my own money, and I was an adult who could afford to treat her family to dinner.

Okay, so the truth was that I was on my own now, and I was an adult with a hot, rich boyfriend who offered to let her look like she was doing well enough to treat her family to a nice dinner at a Beverly Hills hot-spot.

That's exactly what Max had done, and why he'd done it.

My dad didn't look happy for the entire meal. In fact, he didn't say much at all.

Mom, though, seemed to have developed a knack for surreptitiously glancing around the room looking for famous people. I'd heard that Spago was a good place for celebrity spotting, but it looked like we picked the wrong night.

That is, until a large entourage entered the place and people starting looking to see who it was. Turns out it was Linda Evans, an actress who starred on one of my mom's favorite prime-time soaps, *Dynasty*. I'd never seen it. It was before my time. But mom was happy to tell us all about it, and we let her go on and on because she looked so star-struck and elated. Dad told us it had ruined many a baseball game for him—my mom would insist that they switch the channel for that hour, and they only had the one TV.

"Do you think we'll see Krystal?" Grace asked.

"Doubt it. But let me see."

I got my phone out and texted her to warn her that we'd be stopping by the apartment. She texted back and said she was going to the movies with a friend. I briefly worried about whether that was true—she'd been doing well all week, getting ready for the big change—but I had my own things to handle at the moment.

"Krystal's at work again. She works so much," I said, taking a big bite of my entrée.

I couldn't wait to get home and go to sleep. All the deceit was wearing me out.

ELEVEN

I was nervous leading the way up to my apartment. The way things were with Krystal, there was no telling what we might walk in on. She could be sitting there perfectly normal, having found a bit of courage to see Grace and my parents. Or she could be on the den floor, having a threesome or a full-fledged orgy for that matter.

But it appeared she wasn't there. The apartment was dark, except for the lights over the island in the kitchen, shedding enough illumination for me as I turned on the lamps in the den.

"Well, this is it." I shrugged. "Not very big, I know, but by LA standards this is huge."

My dad frowned. Mom immediately asked why we didn't have curtains on the windows and I pictured a day when I'd get a UPS package with some of her homemade curtains that were suitable only for people over sixty. Grace said she liked the place.

It was then that I noticed a flower arrangement on the coffee table. I picked it up, looked at the card, and saw that it just had a hand-drawn heart on it. Maybe someone had given them to Krystal. Or maybe it was from Max and Krystal had put them there so I wouldn't miss them. I couldn't tell, either way, without there being any handwriting.

We weren't there even five minutes before there was a knock at the door. It was two people, a guy and a girl, who said they were Krystal's friends—I'd never met them before—and they said she didn't show up for dinner and the movie was starting soon, and did I know where she was?

"No. She told me she was going out. Did you call or text her?"

The guy nodded.

The girl said, "She's not answering."

They had a look of concern on their faces that I knew was probably matched by mine.

"Everything okay?" Mom called out from the den.

"Yeah, just a sec."

I stepped outside and closed the door behind me.

"You guys know she's in kind of a bad place, right?"

"Yeah. She told us everything," the girl said. "We're not part of that same crowd."

"Okay, good. But I bet that's who she's with."

"We'll go looking around at the usual spots," the guy said.

The girl told me her name was Molly; the guy was Kevin. I hated even hearing that name now.

I said, "I'd go with you but my family is here visiting. If you find her, let me know."

We exchanged numbers, and they went on their way.

My parents and Grace stayed about an hour or so. Most of the time was spent focused on the baby, which was great in so many ways, not the least of which was that it closed off a lot of opportunities for my parents to resume their campaign to bring me home with them.

Although, Mom tried in her own not-so-subtle way. She brought up things that she thought would make me homesick.

Each time, Dad would say something like, "But you'd know that if were you were still home."

I was getting frustrated with this. So much so that I couldn't keep it inside anymore.

"This *is* my home. You're looking at it."

They looked surprised.

"Olivia..." Grace said in a pleading tone, her voice trailing off.

"What, Grace?" I snapped, then looked back at my parents. "I'm living here now. I've started my life. I'm happy, okay? Really happy. And you should be happy for me."

"You're right," my mom said with a look on her face that told me she was simply trying to put an end to this little spat.

Dad, for once, didn't say anything.

The baby started to cry. Grace gathered her up and checked her diaper.

Mom said, "Does she need to be changed?"

"No," Grace said. "I think she needs a nap. Can we get going?"

The tension was heavy. I hated it. Hated every second of it. What had started out as a relatively nice weekend was turning out exactly as I had feared. The bickering, passive-aggressiveness, control—all of it, everything I had left behind in Ohio—was now in my den in my new home.

I just wanted them to leave.

And as they did, we made half-hearted plans to have breakfast before they hit the road the next morning.

I tried calling Krystal when they were gone. No answer. I left a voicemail, then texted her. I was becoming increasingly convinced that she was off with the "friends" who had the cocaine.

I called Max.

"Hello, dream girl," he answered.

"Can you come over?"

"What's wrong? Where's the family?"

I felt the sting in back of my throat that I get just before I cry. But I fought it back. "My family's gone back to their hotel, and *they're* what's wrong."

"Oh no. I'm sorry."

"Can you just please come over here? I need you."

"Give me thirty minutes."

My phone served as a good time-killer while I waited for Max. I checked Twitter to see what was up with the people I was following, and the trending topics. Nothing much interested me. So I opened the browser and went to People magazine, where they had photos from the red carpet at the Emmys.

I thought about that night Max took me to the movie premier in New York City. My first red carpet event. Maybe my last, too. But I didn't care. Seeing how extraordinarily glamorous the women looked made me feel like a poser by comparison. I had no business even thinking I could pull that off.

I snapped out of my downward spiral thinking when I heard a key in the door. It was either Krystal, or it could be Max, who had a key, but it was a little too early for that. He'd said to give him thirty minutes.

I stayed on the couch but looked at the door as the knob turned slowly. Krystal sneaking in, I thought.

Then I froze. My mouth went dry. My eyes widened and stayed there.

Holy fuck. Chris….

TWELVE

I sat in shock on the couch as he crossed the threshold of my apartment.

He held up one hand. "It's okay," he said in a calm voice.

I shot up to my feet. "Get the fuck out!"

He closed the door and locked it without turning around. He faced me the whole time. His expression was serious, intense, crazy....

Luckily I had my phone in my hand. I raised it to dial 911.

Chris rushed me. I didn't have time to evade his quick movement. His arms wrapped around me, bear-hugging me from the side, almost crushing me. With one hand, he tried to pry the phone away from me, but I clutched it like my life depended on it because it probably did.

He was breathing heavily through clenched teeth, and I felt his saliva spraying against my cheek when he exhaled.

"Help! Get the *fuck away* from me! Help!"

"Give it up."

"Let me go! *Help me*!"

He squeezed me tighter, almost so I couldn't breathe, and said, "Did you like my flowers, sweetheart?"

Holy fuck fuck fuck!

He'd been in my house. How? Where did he get a key?

I needed to breathe. My face was getting tingly and I could hear my heart racing in my ears. He was still gripping me from the side, so as best I could I gathered all the strength in my body and forced my leg up and to the side, slamming into him—right into his balls.

He made a sound like "Ooomph" and released me. He staggered back a couple of steps, bent over, his hand between his legs.

I'd never taken a self-defense class before, and I'd never even thought about what I might do in situations like this. So maybe what I did next just came naturally. Or maybe from the movies.

I kicked him in the face. The bottom part of my shoe connected with his forehead and the short but thick heel caught his chin. I heard his jaw snap shut with a sickening and loud sound.

He tried to say something, but couldn't. Blood rushed from his mouth in a torrent. He opened his mouth as I stood over him, again trying to say something. His gaping maw was a deep, dark red, but I could tell his two front teeth were gone.

Adrenaline was flowing intensely through me. I could have killed him. Easily.

I moved closer to him, and he made one more attempt to fight, grabbing my ankle.

I raised my other leg and brought down my foot. A hard, crushing stomp on his crotch.

Chris turned on his side, curling up in the fetal position. Blood gushed from his mouth and it started forming a pool on the carpet.

I miraculously still had the phone in my hand. I swiped the lock screen, touched the dialer, and then the Emergency icon at the top.

Chris wasn't going anywhere.

The 911 operator answered and I spluttered out a nearly incomprehensible string of words.

"Ma'am, slow down. Please calm down. Do you need police?"

"Yesyesyesyes...."

The police arrived quickly. It must have only been four or five minutes. I had opened the door in the meantime, and I had also moved one of the chairs closer to Chris, where I stood on it, trapping his legs underneath.

When I saw the first officer come through the door, I jumped off the chair and collapsed on the couch. The adrenaline rush was subsiding and I just felt like I wanted to sleep. Forever.

I called Max. "Where are you?"

"About five minutes away. Why? What's wrong?"

I was crying again.

"Olivia," he said, flatly. "What is it?"

"J-j-just get here."

It didn't take him five minutes. Probably closer to three. I was sitting in the back of an ambulance when I saw him pull up. They were checking me out because my left side hurt like hell.

They were loading Chris on to another ambulance.

"Max!" I called out, which only made me hurt more.

He turned, saw me, and rushed over through the flashing blue, white and red lights.

"Please stand back, sir," one of the paramedics said.

"That's my girlfriend. What happened, Olivia?"

The paramedic who was checking me out broke in. “We’re going to take you to the hospital. Your ribs need to be x-rayed.”

“Jesus, Olivia. Will someone tell me what happened?”

Across the parking lot, we heard some shouting and lots of movement followed. I looked and saw that they’d found Chris’s car.

The only words I heard were “keys” and “crowbar.”

Then more commotion.

Max and I watched in horror as the cops popped open the trunk of Chris’s car and pulled Krystal out of it.

She had duct tape wrapped around her head, covering her mouth, but not her nose. Her hair was a wreck and when the white light shone on her, I could see a welt on the side of her face.

I wanted to pass out. Maybe die right there.

“Let’s go,” the paramedic said, and Max jumped in the back of the ambulance.

“I’m riding with her.”

“Wait. I want to see Krystal.”

The paramedic closed the back doors of the ambulance. “We’ll find out how she’s doing, ma’am.”

“Olivia,” Max said sternly, “what the fuck is happening?”

I told him on the way to the hospital.

THIRTEEN

I was in an ER examination room, waiting for them to take a look at my x-rays. The doctor was pretty sure I had broken at least one rib, but wanted to take a look and see how bad the damage was.

Max went to get an update on Krystal and came back about fifteen minutes later with the news that other than the contusion on her cheek, she was going to be fine. At least as far as injuries went. She would be released that night, and Max had promised the doctor she was going straight to a rehab center in Beverly Hills. He said the doctor knew right away that she had a problem. She'd been exhibiting early symptoms of withdrawal.

The next thing to worry about: my parents. Call them right away? Wait until morning?

Max said to wait until the morning. "They'll be leaving tomorrow. Let them sleep."

"They'll be pissed."

"Do you think they'll want to stay longer now?"

I sighed. "I don't know. I don't want them to have to do that. Oh, God. We had a fight last night." I told him all about it.

When I was finished filling him in he said, "Call them."

He was right. It was the right thing to do.

He handed me my phone and I called Grace.

"Oh my God!" she yelled, when I told her where I was and why.

"Grace. Calm down. I'm going to be fine. I just need you to go wake Mom and Dad. You guys can come down here."

"Okay. Okay." She was almost breathless.

"Grace?"

"Yeah?"

"I'm going to be fine. Make sure you tell them that."

Sometimes I had to be the more controlled, mature one between us.

While we waited for them to arrive, I gave a statement to the police. I was nervous at first, but the pain killers were really starting to kick in. Plus, the officer who interviewed me looked really sympathetic to what had happened to me.

"Was there any sexual contact with the assailant?" the officer asked.

Max looked at me and lowered his head, looking at the floor. He hadn't asked me that, and I guess he was feeling some guilt over it. I reached out and grabbed his wrist.

"No."

Max let out a heavy sigh and squeezed my hand back.

"I think we have all we need for now," the cop said. "Do you have any questions for me?"

Max blurted: "Where is he?"

"Being fixed up as best they can here. Then he's off to jail. There'll be an arraignment Monday morning, most likely."

I said, "Do I have to be there?"

"No, ma'am."

I thought for a moment. "What's going to happen to him?"

"Well," the officer said, putting his pen back in his shirt pocket, "the assault on you will carry a good bit of time. But the major thing is the kidnapping."

"Kidnapping?"

"Yes, ma'am. When he took your roommate—what's her name... Ms. Sherman?"

I nodded.

"That was kidnapping," the officer said. "And that carries hefty time. It'll be years before he sees the outside of a prison again."

"Good," Max said.

And then an awkward moment happened. The cop recognized Max and gushed over his movies. Max was gracious about it, and the cop didn't go on too long, or ask for an autograph or anything else. He just shook Max's hand and said, "If there's anything you or your girlfriend need, give me a call." He gave Max his card, Max thanked him, and the cop was gone.

It was a disaster when my parents got there. In their minds, their worst nightmare had come true and their suspicions and fears about LA were confirmed.

My mom ran over to try to hug me, but I had to fend her off because it would have hurt. Dad kissed my forehead. Grace cried and hugged my legs.

"Tell me what happened," Dad said.

I recounted the whole story for them, and they stood there in shock. Chris? The guy they thought would be and *should be* my future husband did this?

Why, yes. Yes, he did.

"It's my fault," Grace kept saying.

The whole sordid story came out. And I told my parents everything.

I also told them about Max, who had offered to leave the room for a little while so I could see my family without having to explain who he was right away. He said he'd be down in the hospital cafeteria and for me to text him when I wanted him to come back.

"Olivia," Mom said, "why haven't you been truthful with us?"

I rolled my eyes. "You know why. Ninety percent of our conversations are about how I've made the wrong decision. About my major in college, about moving to LA, everything."

She started to say something.

I stopped her. "Let me finish. Please. For once. Look, I understand why you guys doubt what I'm doing. I get it. You care about me. But it's too much. Way too much. And all this time you've been worried about something happening to me out here, the only time it did was when someone from back home came all the way out here, like a crazy person, to hurt me."

I looked at them and let that sink in.

Mercifully, the doctor came into the room at that point.

"Well, I see we have the whole family here." He said it almost cheerily, which I kind of liked. There's nothing worse than a doctor with a grim bedside manner.

The doctor introduced himself to my parents and then asked me if I wanted to go over the x-rays alone.

"We're her parents," my father said.

"Yes, but she's an adult. I can't discuss her medical issues around anyone else without her permission."

"It's okay," I said. I really just wanted to get it over with and get out of there.

The doctor confirmed that I had one broken rib.

"Nothing much to do for it. Just rest and some pain medication."

Everyone looked relieved.

The doctor continued: "Do you live with your parents?"

"No."

"Alone?"

"No. Well, I have a roommate, but—"

"I gotcha," the doctor said. "Sorry, I forgot for a minute. It's been a little crazy here tonight. It might be a good idea if you stayed with your parents." He looked at them. "Just to make sure she's okay for the next couple of days. Nothing major."

"We don't live here," Dad said. I noticed his voice was softer. He sounded almost as if he had become resigned to the idea that I was on my own.

"And we're supposed to leave to go home today," Mom said.

Grace was holding the baby, who was sleeping, and whispered, "Maybe we should stay."

"It's okay," I said. "I know what I can do."

FOURTEEN

Max walked into the hospital room a few minutes after I texted him.

He was a gentleman, referring to my parents as Mrs. Rowland and Mr. Rowland, and telling Grace it was a pleasure to meet her. He stuck is finger out like he was going to poke my baby niece but instead she grabbed on to it.

I think after telling my parents about Max they had the idea that when he got to the room, he'd walk in with an entourage and paparazzi snapping pictures. I'm pretty sure they were expecting him to walk in and be flashy, arrogant, aloof, and all the other clichés people associate with Hollywood.

But Max, as always, couldn't have been more down to earth, and I think that threw them for a loop.

"I'm sorry I couldn't have gotten there sooner after Olivia called," he said to my family.

Before anyone else could respond I said, "You're not Batman, you know."

He flashed me his smile.

My parents laughed for the first time in…well, as long as I could remember.

He was only there a few minutes before my dad said, "Mind if we talk out in the hall?"

Max didn't hesitate. "Not at all."

As the two left the room, I thought: *Oh, no. My dad's going to chase him off. Probably try to talk Max into taking their side in the debate over whether I should go back home to Ohio.*

But Max wouldn't do that, I knew. Still, it was probably going to be uncomfortable for him, and I hated that thought.

Grace said, "Wow. Just…wow."

My mother looked at her. "What's wow?"

Grace's mouth fell open. "Uh, hello, Mother? Did you not see how hot Olivia's boyfriend is?"

For the first time in my life, I saw a look on my mother's face that she probably wished she would never let her daughters see. It was just the slightest raising of the eyebrows, and the corner of her mouth turned up a little.

"Looks aren't as important as what's on the inside," Mom said. She looked at me.

Grace looked at me, waiting for me to defend Max, probably expecting me to rattle off a list of all of his good qualities.

But I didn't. I just said, "I love him. I do. I really do."

I started to tear up. My mom came to the bedside and put her hand on mine and just smiled.

My parents met with the doctor again and he reassured them that my injury was minor, and that I'd be fine.

While they were talking with the doctor in the hall, Grace said she was going to change the baby's diaper somewhere. Max and I had a few moments alone.

"What did you and my dad talk about?"

He was rubbing my forearm. "Mostly football. He wanted to know who I had in the Super Bowl."

"Shut up."

Max smiled. "No. Really, it was a good talk. He told me he wasn't happy with you being here, but he knew you were going to do what you wanted."

"I wish he'd admit that to my face."

"Yeah," Max said, "well, take what you can get. He asked me where I was from, things like that. I think he liked the fact that I'm a Midwesterner."

I rolled my eyes. "He can be kind of territorial like that."

"Did you tell them about leaving the agency?"

I shook my head.

"Didn't think so," he said. "Because your dad looked kind of surprised when I told him you were going to be my assistant and editor."

My eyebrows shot up my head. "Editor?"

"Well, yeah. First reader, gatekeeper. Honest with me when I write something shitty."

I just smiled. This was going to be so good.

"He also asked what my intentions were with you."

I laughed and covered my mouth.

"Not like *that*," he said. "But don't you think for a second that it ever leaves my mind."

"Even when I'm looking like this? Like shit?"

He shook his head. "You're always gorgeous."

"So do I get to go home with you?"

"That's another thing he wanted to know. If I'd look after you. I told him yes, and not just until you're healed."

My emotions were over the top. There was no controlling them. I needed to tell him how I felt. I needed to see the look on his face when I told him. And I needed to do it before he went through with the promises he'd made to my father.

"I love you."

Those three words. Three powerful words. The three words I needed to say to him. But they hadn't come out of my mouth. They came out of his. Suddenly. Without warning. Right at the time I was going to say that to him. Once again, it was like he could read my mind.

"Come closer and kiss me," I said.

Max leaned over and placed his lips gently on mine.

Through our kiss I said a somewhat muffled, "I love you. I love you. I've loved you for a while now."

We heard the door handle click and Max pulled away.

FIFTEEN

Two weeks later, on a Saturday afternoon, I woke from a nap to the sound of my phone ringing. It was my parents checking in. They had called every day for the last two weeks.

Conversations with my parents had changed for the better. No arguing. No bickering. No hassling me over my life choices. They even talked to Max a couple of times. Short conversations, and from what I could hear on his end, they were mostly trying to get him to confirm the progress I was making health-wise.

I wasn't one-hundred percent healed, but I was feeling much better. The pain-killers played a big part in that, too.

When I talked to Grace, she asked about Krystal.

"She's been in rehab for two weeks. I haven't gone to visit her and she's not allowed to have her own phone, but she called a couple of days ago and sounded really good."

"I heard her parents are there."

"Yeah, she said that. They were trying to get her transferred but she's not covered by insurance, so she's staying here."

Grade said, "Max paid for it all?"

"Yeah."

"You better not let him get away."

Max had laid down with me, but he was no longer in the bed. I thought maybe he'd gone for a run.

I made my way from his bedroom—*our* bedroom, now that I was living with him permanently—down the stairs and into the large, open den. The view outside was gorgeous. A bright, clear day in Los Angeles. A rare event, to say the least.

Max was sitting in a large leather chair with his feet up on an ottoman. He had a sheaf of papers in his hand, and a blue editing pen in the other. His laptop was on the coffee table. I stood there at the foot of the stairs for a few minutes, watching the man I love engrossed in the work he loved so much.

He did a double-take when he noticed me standing there.

"How long have you been there?" he said.

"Just a couple of minutes."

"Well, come here."

I walked over to him. He put the script aside and held out his arms, lowering me onto his lap.

Both of us were still in our nap-wear. He wore just a pair of cotton workout shorts. I had on a t-shirt and panties.

Max kissed my check. "How are you feeling?"

"You mean since the last time you asked me two hours ago?"

He kissed my neck, and I felt him getting hard beneath my thigh. Max had been strict about my recovery, not letting me do anything strenuous, which included sex. So we'd been on a two-week run of celibacy. It kind of amazed me that we pulled it off.

"In fact," I continued as he kept nuzzling my neck, "you've asked me every couple of hours for two weeks."

"I'm just playing doctor."

I moaned. "Now, that sounds like fun." And then something occurred to me. "Are you asking purely for medical reasons, or are you just waiting for me to say I'm feeling well enough for you to make love to me?"

"Am I that transparent?"

I laughed.

He said, "Both, actually. You got me."

I turned my head to face him, and pressed my lips to his. We had kissed during the two weeks, but this was different. Deeper. Passionate. Wanting. Needing.

"Switch places with me," he said.

He remembered I had said that, for whatever reason, I felt better and more comfortable when I was sitting up.

He lifted me gently and stood, then placed me back down on the chair. He tugged on my panties, and I wiggled as best I could to help him get them down my legs.

"I've missed this, Liv," he said, lowering his head between my legs and licking me. I was already wet from sitting on his lap and feeling his erection growing under me.

I looked down and watched him caressing my cleft with his tongue. "I've missed it, too."

Max wasn't in the mood to put this off any longer. He brought his head up, and stayed kneeling on the floor. I was sitting on the edge of the chair—we were lined up perfectly for what both of us had been longing for.

Max pulled down the front of his shorts, exposing his beautiful cock. I reached down, needing to touch him. He was fully hard, and warm, and I could almost swear I felt his pulse in the veins of his length.

He pushed forward a little, and I guided him to me.

"I'll go slow," he said.

"Do whatever you want."

"Maybe later, when you're really ready. But I admire your enthusiasm."

"Max?" I said, raising my eyebrows.

"Yeah."

"Stop talking."

He pushed the head of his cock into me. But only that far. He moved his hips back and forth, sliding into me a little more each time. Shallow, slow thrusts.

What had been two weeks felt more like two years without him inside me.

I put my hand on his chest. He had a hand on each of my hips.

Max leaned forward and our lips met. My tongue darted into his mouth, and he sucked on it, the way that turned me on so much. Then I took his tongue between my lips, turning my head from side to side as my mouth slid back and forth on his tongue as if I were giving him a blowjob.

Our eyes were open the whole time. Locked in a deep stare. It didn't even seem like we were blinking.

When I freed his tongue, he said, "I almost forgot how tight you are."

"It's been too long."

"Much too long."

Max looked down and my gaze followed his. Together we watched him disappear inside me. He was deep now, almost too deep—but only because it made my breath hitch and little stabs of dull pain shot through my healing bones.

I winced.

Max stopped. "You okay?"

"Don't stop. Don't stop."

Max pushed in again—not deep strokes, and not as fast as he'd started doing it just before the pain…slow, even thrusts.

"I'm gonna come," he said.

"Do it."

"Come with me, Liv."

I started to climax, feeling the surge building quickly. It had been so long. Too long for Max, too. I felt the hot, thick spurts flooding me, and it made his slow thrusts even slicker.

He held my hips tight. I wrapped my arms around his neck and pressed my face into his shoulder, biting him gently as I came with him.

EPILOGUE

It's been two years since that happened.

I ended up not having to testify in Chris's trial. He took a plea bargain and got a nineteen year sentence. I'd always liked his parents and they'd always liked me, but there was still something strange about receiving a letter from them, apologizing for their son's actions. They didn't have my address, but they'd given it to Grace and she'd sent it to me.

The last I heard, Kevin's agency died a slow death. After shooting Max's last movie, Jacqueline Mathers moved to another agency. Word got out that Kevin got drunk one night and tried to pressure her into sex, so he was pretty much finished. I have no idea what he's doing now.

Krystal completed her rehab and is now living back in our hometown in Ohio. Grace recently told me that Krystal is pregnant and there's a hastily planned wedding in the works. I'm sure we'll go, and I'm fairly sure I'll be in her wedding. After all, she was in mine just over a year ago.

I'm not sure when Max and I will have another child, but we've talked about it. Taking care of a baby is enough work for one person, let alone two people who work from home all the time.

After his last movie, Max stopped producing and directing. He's now writing full-time, and I've never seen him happier. We go to his mother's house once a month for Sunday dinner. She does it just like back home—there's nothing like a traditional meal cooked by mom—and she can't get enough of her little grandson.

Max has sold two scripts and is working on a new one now. I haven't told him yet, but I don't like it as much as the last two. But I'll tell him. I'm brutally honest with him, and he always accepts my suggestions.

I love reading his work. The characters and stories that come out of his mind always amaze me.

I often think how all of this started one day when I was a sophomore in college and decided I wanted to work in Hollywood in some capacity.

That girl—the young me—made a fateful decision back then, bucking her parents' objections, and going against all their advice for years to come. I couldn't have imagined in a thousand years that it would work out this way.

I also think a lot about what Max said after I read that script he left me when he made an effort to open up to me after the tabloid scandal. I remember his words verbatim:

"I've never believed in fate," he said. "But honestly, when I was writing that—specifically her character—it was different from all the other things I'd ever written before. Or since, actually. I've always had to work on characters for a long time, getting them right, changing things about them. But she was different. She just…came to me…out of nowhere, already perfect. Just like you."

His words back then made my heart melt. I knew he meant them.

But in the time since, we've both learned that neither of us is perfect. What we are, though, is perfect for each other.

One day recently I asked him if he still doesn't believe in fate.

"I don't know anymore. But I do think almost anything's possible. Things are just waiting out there and if you have a moment of courage, you put your fear aside and go for it."

That's exactly what we've been doing all this time.

I had come halfway across the country to find the love of my life, and I didn't even know I was doing it. It wasn't an easy path, but then nothing worth having is easy. I'd have gone through even more difficult and dangerous things to find Max, and I know he would have done the same for me.

"Things are better when they're not scripted, anyway," he said. "Fate would mean it's scripted."

"Strange thing for a writer to say."

He pondered that for a moment. "Yeah, but that's fiction." He paused. "This is real."

And so it is.

Get in touch, get updates, and special announcements from Kate!

Web: **katedawes.com**

Twitter: **@katedawes**

Made in the USA
Lexington, KY
21 September 2014